FROM THE BOOKS OF
Jane Wilson

The next day's recitations hastily prepared, the
Lookouts had gathered in Ronny's room for a spread.
(*Marjorie Dean, College Freshman*) *Page 207*

MARJORIE DEAN
COLLEGE FRESHMAN

By PAULINE LESTER

Author of
*"Marjorie Dean, College Sophomore," "Marjorie Dean,
College Junior," "Marjorie Dean, College Senior,"*
and
The Marjorie Dean High School Series

A. L. BURT COMPANY
Publishers   New York

THE
Marjorie Dean College Series

A Series of Stories for Girls 12 to 18 Years of Age

By PAULINE LESTER

Marjorie Dean, College Freshman
Marjorie Dean, College Sophomore
Marjorie Dean, College Junior
Marjorie Dean, College Senior

MARJORIE DEAN, COLLEGE FRESHMAN

CHAPTER I.

A LONELY LOOKOUT.

"OH, dear! I wish Jerry would come home! I want to see her! I've always missed her terribly during vacations, but this summer I've missed her more than ever. I'm simply starved for a sight of her dear jolly face! Here it is, the twenty-fourth of August, and no Jerry Jeremiah Geraldine Macy!"

Marjorie Dean had addressed this little series of wistful remarks to no one in particular. She stood at one of the long French windows of the living room, her nose flattened against the pane, little-girl fashion, watching a very wet outdoors. All morning the rain had been beating down with a sullen persistency which Marjorie found distinctly disheartening. She was as near to having a case of the blues as was possible to one of her care-free, buoyant nature. Wet weather did not often interfere

3

with her happiness. Given her particular girl
friends within telephone call and she could discount
a rainy day.

Today she was without that source of entertain-
ment and consolation. None of her chums had
returned to Sanford from their summer outings.
Susan Atwell, Irma Linton, Muriel Harding, Constance Stevens, Jerry Macy—all were missing from
the town into which Marjorie had come, a stranger,
but of which she now was, to use her own expression, "a regular citizen."

Marjorie's thoughts were dwelling on her absent
schoolmates as she pensively watched the rain. She
wondered if, wherever they were, they were penned
in by the rain too. It seemed rather queer to her
that she should be the only one of the sextette of
girls, who had founded the Lookout Club, to be
spending the summer in Sanford. She was not a
real Sanfordite by birth. With the exception of
Constance Stevens, the others claimed Sanford as
their native town.

Readers of the "MARJORIE DEAN HIGH SCHOOL
SERIES" have already an acquaintance with Marjorie Dean, and have followed her course as a student at Sanford High School. They have seen her
through both sad and happy days, the events of
which have been chronicled in "MARJORIE DEAN,
HIGH SCHOOL FRESHMAN," "MARJORIE DEAN,

High School Sophomore," "Marjorie Dean, High School Junior," and "Marjorie Dean, High School Senior."

"There goes that old mail carrier and he isn't going to stop here!" This time Marjorie's tones were not wistful. Their disgusted energy indicated her patent disappointment. Her red lips drooped in dejection as she saw the unfeeling object of her hopeful anticipation plod stolidly past the gate without so much as a glance at the mailbox at the foot of the driveway.

"Not one single solitary letter," mourned the watcher. "Why doesn't Jerry write?"

"When did you hear from Jerry last, Lieutenant?" Mrs. Dean had entered the room in time to hear Marjorie's plaint.

"Oh, Captain, I'm *so* glad you came to the rescue! I was *so* lonely! You asked me when last I heard from Jerry. Why, it's almost two weeks. She wrote me it was awfully hot at the beach and—'Are you going to stay here awhile and talk to me, Captain?"

Marjorie interrupted herself with this question. Her downcast face had begun to brighten.

"If you are," she continued, "I'll run up to my house and get Jerry's last letter. I'd love to read it to you."

"I'll oblige you by staying awhile." Mrs. Dean sat down in her own particular wicker rocker, her eyes resting fondly on Marjorie.

"You're a dear. Be back in a minute." A rush of light feet on the stairs proclaimed that Marjorie had gone to her "house," as she chose to call her pretty pink and white room, for her letter.

"I can't find it," presently announced a disappointed voice from above stairs. "Have you seen a square gray envelope with large writing on it anywhere in the living room, Captain?"

"I am looking straight at one now," came the reassuring information. "You left it on the mantelpiece, Lieutenant."

"Oh, thank you." A moment and Marjorie was heard making a vigorous descent of the stairs.

"I came down stairs at a positive gallop," she said lightly, as she crossed the room and secured her letter. "I was afraid I had left it in the table drawer in the pagoda. If I had, that would have meant a wading trip for me. I suppose I'd have gone after it, but I am glad it's here."

"You are overflowing with repressed energy, Marjorie," Mrs. Dean said, looking a trifle anxious. "I wonder if a quiet summer at home has really been best for you. While there is no place I know more comfortable than our own home, the change would have been beneficial to you. I believe we should have spent, at least, two weeks at the beach or in the mountains."

"Please don't feel that you haven't done the very best for me, Captain!" was Marjorie's instant response. "You know it was my fault that we didn't go away this vacation. I said I had rather stay at home. We didn't care to go anywhere for an outing without General, and, so long as he couldn't be with us, we decided that home was nicest. That's the way things were. How can you say you were to blame?"

Marjorie was hanging over her mother's chair now, soft hands patting the face she loved most in the world.

"I wanted particularly to be at home this summer on account of my going to college in the fall. Ever since we came to Sanford to live I have had one long succession of good times. Most of them have taken me away from you. If I had a party, then I had to be with my guests. If I was invited to one, that took me away from you."

"But my own dear lieutenant, your captain wished you to have these good times with your school friends," reasoned her mother. "I could hardly expect to keep you tied to my apron string."

"I know you have been the most unselfish mother in the whole world," stoutly asserted Marjorie. "I know I haven't appreciated you half so highly as I ought. It all comes over me now just because it is growing nearer the time to go to college. I can't bear to think about it."

The merry light had faded from Marjorie's features. Her lips had begun to quiver. Her two hands dropped inert to her captain's shoulders and rested there. She had no words for all that was in her heart.

Leaving her captain to go to Hamilton College was bound to be the greatest cross Marjorie had, thus far in her happy young life, been called upon to bear. She always missed her general keenly when he went away on long business trips. This in the warm shelter of her mother's devotion. But to part from Captain! Not to see her every day; not to hear her beloved voice! Marjorie sometimes tried to dwell on this sad feature of entering college. She found it unendurable and frequently entertained the desperate wish that her parents might suddenly discover that they could not afford to send her to college. That would be a legitimate excuse for staying at home.

A brief interval of silence followed her woeful declaration. It was broken by a stifled sob. The little lieutenant had struggled hard to keep back her tears, but had failed. Without a word she bundled herself in to her mother's arms. Heavy showers were due to fall indoors as well as out.

CHAPTER II.

A TALK WITH CAPTAIN AND A SURPRISE.

PRESENTLY clearance came. With a long sigh, Marjorie raised her head. She was just in time to see her mother wiping her own eyes and making a valiant effort to smile. It pulled the little lieutenant together as nothing else could have done.

"Oh, Captain, forgive me!" she cried out in contrition. It was unusual to see tears in her mother's soft eyes. "I'm a nice kind of soldier!"

"No harm done," was the tender response. "This little tear shower was bound to fall, sooner or later. I am all right now." Her mother's wavering smile steadied itself.

"I've tried to keep away from the sad side of going away to college," Marjorie said somberly, "but how many girls are there who have the dear beautiful home life that I have? And this summer alone with you! It's been great happiness and sadness all jumbled together. Every once in awhile when I am very happy, I suddenly remember that there's a shadow. I have to stop for a minute to think what it is. Then I know—I am going away from my captain before long."

"You must also stop to remember that you can't go through life only half educated," practically reminded Mrs. Dean, with a view toward lightening the lieutenant's pessimistic views. "At least, General and I do not propose that you shall. Suppose you wished more than all else to go through college and we could not afford to send you? That would really be a case for lamentation."

"I've thought of all that," Marjorie returned soberly. "I know it is splendid that I have the opportunity. I am thankful for all my benefits, truly I am. I ought to be glad I haven't Lucy Warner's problem to solve."

"I don't believe either General or I could truly accuse you of being ungrateful." Mrs. Dean smiled down upon the flushed face so near her own. "Do you think Lucy Warner will try to enter Hamilton College this fall?" She asked this question with a double object in view. First, to take Marjorie's mind off herself. While on the subject of college, she wished also to draw from Marjorie, if possible, Lucy's present attitude toward the world in general. When, occasionally, Marjorie had entertained Lucy at the house that summer at luncheon or dinner, Mrs. Dean had accorded her the same friendly courtesy she would have extended to Jerry or Muriel. She had never quite forgiven Lucy for the unhappiness she had caused Marjorie during both her junior and senior years at high school. She had not yet come to a point where she could repose faith in the odd, green-eyed girl of whom Marjorie had grown so fond.

"She would like to, but she is worried about the expenses. They are so high at Hamilton." Marjorie's face clouded momentairly. "She could draw whatever sum of money she needs from the Lookouts' treasury, but she won't. I may tell you, Captain, but no one else—Lucy feels dreadfully yet, over that misunderstanding we had last year. She blames herself for not having believed in me. She says the other girls would not have doubted me, and she had no right to be so hard on me. She thinks she isn't worthy of help from the club. She told me this, privately, because she felt it was my right to know."

Mrs. Dean's long-harbored sense of injury against Lucy Warner took sudden flight. She understood at last the peculiar girl's innate honesty of character, and could not do else than respect her for her drastic stand.

"Lucy feels afraid she may not find any kind of work at Hamilton to help her out with her personal expenses," Marjorie continued. "She can tutor in either Latin or mathematics. She has saved nearly two hundred dollars from her work last year and this summer. If she should enter Hamilton this fall her mother will do practical nursing. Then she will be earning quite a good deal of money and she won't be so lonely. That's the way things are with Lucy. I wish she would enter college with the rest of us. It would be easier for her and nice for us to be freshmen together."

"Would Lucy accept financial help from you? You may offer it to her if you think best, Lieutenant." Mrs. Dean's generous proposal arose from a relieved mind. She could make it with absolute freedom of spirit.

"No, Captain. I am the last one Lucy would allow to help her. If Ronny were here she might be able to make Lucy see things in the right light. Ronny is the only one, I feel sure, who could convince her. She would not give up until she had. But goodness knows when we shall see Ronny again!"

An anxious little pucker appeared between Marjorie's brows. Not since the first of July had she heard word from Veronica Lynne, Miss Archer's God-child. Ronny had left Sanford a few days after Commencement, and had written her a lengthy train letter, en route for California. This Marjorie had answered, using a San Francisco address Ronny had given her. For one reason or another, Ronny had not replied to it.

"I wish Ronny would write me," she said. "She

promised me she'd write *me* if she didn't write any-one else. I know she will keep her word; but when?"

During their confidential talk, Marjorie had remained seated on her mother's lap. Tardy recollection that she was altogether too heavy for comfort brought her to her feet.

"Poor, dear Captain!" she exclaimed. "You can't help but be tired from holding a great, heavy elephant like me! We had so much to talk about. I forgot everything except how nice it was to snuggle close to you and be comforted. That's the very hardest part of being away from you. I won't have my superior officers near by to report to."

"You will have to tuck your reports away in your mind and have a reporting session when you come home on your vacations," her mother suggested.

"Yes; and I promise you, Captain, that all my vacations will be spent with *you*." Marjorie pointed an emphatic finger at her mother. "I'll never desert my Captain and my General when I have a furlough. No, sir!"

"I think I shall hold you to that promise, Lieutenant. You have made it of your own accord. I would rather have it a free will promise. You will be away the greater part of the year. Those pre-

cious vacations belong to us. I know General feels
the same."

"I wish you both to be very stingy of me. Then
I shall be sure you love me a lot," Marjorie replied
with playful emphasis. She no longer felt like crying. While outdoors the rain continued to beat
down; indoors the sun had broken through the
clouds.

"Once, oh, very long ago, you spoke of reading
me Jerry's letter," Mrs. Dean presently reminded.
"Then the rain descended and the floods came,
and——"

"We forgot all about it," supplemented Marjorie.
"All right, my dearest Captain, I will proceed to
read it to you this minute." This time she picked
it up from the floor. It had dropped from her hand
when she had briefly descended into the valley of
woe. Settling herself in an easy chair, she unfolded
the letter and promptly began:

" 'Magnificent Marjoram:

" 'I want to go home! It is hot here. This part
of the globe is getting ready to burn down. The
beach is hot; the hotel is hotter and the sun is hot-
test. It was nice and cool here until about a week
ago. Then the sun came rambling along and
started to smile. After that he beamed. Now he is
on the job all day with a broad grin. Maybe we
don't notice it! Still our family love to linger in

this hot berg. Hal hates to give up the bathing. Mother and Father are deep in a series of old-fashioned whist. They meet the same friends here each year, and they always play whist. They are anxious to stay for the last game in the series.

"'I'm the only one who longs for home. I offered to go home by myself and keep Lonesome Hall. Mother said, "Nay, nay!" I pleaded that you would feed and nourish me and let me sleep in your garage until she came home. That didn't go. Here I languish while some of the Macys swim in the surf and others of them hold up a hand at whist.

"'Everyone at Severn Beach is growling about the heat. It has never been like this before. While I'm sitting squarely in front of an electric fan, I'm moderately cool. The minute I move off from it, I'm wilted. The last leaf of the last rose of summer was beautiful as compared to me at the end of a perfect day down here.

"'Next year, we are going to the mountains. I don't know which mountains the folks intend to put up on, but I know where Jeremiah is going. I'm going straight to the top of Mount Everest, which our good old geography used to inform us was the highest peak on earth. Five miles high! Think of it! I shall go clear to the top and roost there all summer. I shall have my meals brought up to me three times a day. That means five miles per meal for somebody. I certainly shall not go after them myself. It will be a wonderful vacation! So restful! Tell you more about it when I see you. You may go along if you happen to need perfect peace and rest.

" 'Oh, Marjorie, I am so anxious to see you and talk my head off! There isn't a single girl at the beach this year that amounts to a handful of popcorn. They are so terribly grown-up and foolish; idiotic I might better say. They make eyes at poor old Hal and he gets so wrathy. Every time he sees one coming towards him, when he is down on the main veranda, you ought to see him arise and vanish. Sometimes, when he gets so disgusted he has to talk, he comes around and tells me how silly he thinks they are. Then, to tease him, I tell him he shouldn't be so beautiful. You ought to hear him rave. If there is anything he hates it is to be called "beautiful."

" 'By the way, how are you enjoying this letter? Great, isn't it? I am trying to tell you all the news, only there is none to tell. Oh, I almost forgot. I must tell you of the lovely walk I had one day last week. I came in from bathing one morning and thought I would take a walk around the town. It had been raining early in the morning and then had grown quite cool for this furnace.

" 'I dressed up in a new white pongee suit, which

is very becoming to Jeremiah, and I wore my best round white hemp hat. It is imported and cost money.

" 'I started out and walked briskly up one avenue and briskly down another. Fast walking is supposed to be good exercise for people who weigh one hundred and forty pounds, when they are hoping to weigh one twenty-five. I won't speak of myself. The streets of this town were paved just after paving was invented, as an advertisement, I suspect, and they have never been touched since. With this explanation, as Miss Flint was fond of remarking, I will proceed with my story.

" 'I was about half way across one of these ancient, hobblety-gobble outrages, when I came to grief. My feet slipped on a slimy brick and I landed flat on my back in a puddle of dirty water. I hit my poor head an awful bang. I'm speaking of myself all right enough now. I was so mad I couldn't think of anything to say. All my choicest slang flew away when I whacked my head. My nice round hemp hat was saved a ducking. It jumped off my head and almost across the street. Some little jumper, that hat! An obliging breeze caught it, and it scuttled off around the corner and would have been home ahead of me if it hadn't collided with a horse block. It sat down with a flop and waited for me.

" 'The spectators to Jeremiah's fall were three children, a horse, and an old green and yellow parrot. The kiddies weren't impressed, but the parrot yelled and ha-ha-ed and enjoyed himself a whole lot. He was in a cage hung on a porch right near where I fell. I don't know what the horse thought. He behaved like a gentleman, though. He didn't either rubber or laugh. That's more than I can say of the other witnesses to my disaster.

" 'But, on with my narrative. I'll leave you to imagine how I looked. My white pongee suit was no longer suitable. It was a disgrace to the noble house of Macy. I had to get home, just the same, so I faced about and hit up a pace for the hotel. I had gone about two blocks when I met a jitney. I never enjoyed meeting anyone so much before as that jitney man. Of course the hotel verandas were full of people. It was just before luncheon and folks were sitting around, hopefully waiting for the dining rooms to open.

" 'Fortunately it was my back that had suffered injury from the mud. I gave one look to see who was behind me. There was no one but an old man in a wheel chair and a couple of spoons. They were so busy beaming on each other that I was a blank to them. I made a dash for the side entrance to the hotel and caught the elevator going up. I went with it. Thus ends the tale of Jeremiah's fateful

walk. Thus ends my news also. When you hear
from me again, it will probably be in person. I
shall hit the trail for Sanford, first chance I have.
I must stop now and go to dinner. I send you the
faithful devotion of a loyal Lookout. That is no
mean little dab of affection. Remember me to your
mother and pat Ruffle for me. Now that I'm ending this letter, I can think of a lot of things to tell
you. Oh, well, I'll write 'em another day or else
say 'em.

" 'Lovingly your friend,
" 'Jerry Macy.' "

Marjorie had stopped reading to laugh more than
once at Jerry's droll phrasing. "Isn't Jerry funny,
Mother?" she exclaimed. "Hal is funny, too. Still
he isn't so funny as Jerry. I think——"

Whatever Marjorie might have further said regarding Jerry's letter remained unspoken. Her
gaze chancing to travel to a window, she sprang to
her feet with an exclamation of surprise. Next she
ran to the window and peered curiously out. A
taxicab from the station had stopped before the
gate. From the house it was not easy to distin-
guish, through the driving rain, the identity of the
solitary fare, for whom the driver had left his
machine to open the gate. It was a slim girlish
figure, too slender to be Jerry. Through the mist
Marjorie caught the smart lines of a navy blue rain

coat, buttoned to the chin and a gleam of bright hair under a tight-lined blue hat.

Could it be? Marjorie's heart began a tattoo of joy. It didn't seem possible—yet the blue-clad figure, making for the house at a run, was unmistakable.

"Captain, it's Ronny!" she shrieked in a high jubilant treble. "She just got out of a taxicab and she's here!"

Without stopping to make further explanation, Marjorie rushed to the front door to welcome the last person she had expected to see on that stormy morning, Veronica Lynne.

CHAPTER III.

THE REAL RONNY.

"RONNY LYNNE, who would have expected to see you?" rejoiced Marjorie. "I can't believe my own eyes." Two welcoming arms embraced the beloved visitor, regardless of her dripping rain coat.

"Oh, I know I'm the great unexpected," laughed Veronica, warmly returning Marjorie's embrace. "Now break away, reckless child, before you are quite as wet as I. See what you get for hugging a rushing rivulet. Oh, Marjorie Dean, but I'm glad to see you! I can't begin to tell you how much I have missed you. I received your letter and meant to answer at once. Then I——"

Veronica broke off in her abrupt fashion. This time it was to greet Mrs. Dean, who, after leaving the two girls together during the first enthusiasm of meeting had now come forward to welcome Ronny.

"A bad day for traveling, but a happy one for us," she said, as she affectionately kissed Miss Archer's God-child. "Help Ronny out of that wet rain coat, Lieutenant. Better go straight upstairs with Marjorie, Veronica. She will soon make you comfortable with one of her negligees and house slippers. I will bring you a cup of consommé. I know you must be hungry."

"I am hungry, and I would love to dress up in some of Marjorie's clothes," Ronny made reply. Marjorie was already busy undoing the buttons of her friend's coat.

"Come right along upstairs then," Marjorie invited. "I'll soon have you fixed all nice and comfy. I am so happy, Ronny. I've been thinking of you as away off in California, and here you have been hustling across the continent to visit me."

"And all the time I have been congratulating

myself on the blessed fact that I would really have
a chance to be chummy with you when I finally
arrived," exulted Ronny, as she ran lightly up the
wide open staircase behind her hostess. Mrs. Dean
had already hurried kitchenward to see to the consommé.

"We will be the best chums ever!" Pausing on
the top step, Marjorie stretched forth a hand.
"Welcome to my house and heart," she said. Tucking her friend's hand within her arms she drew her
down a short hall and into her own particular
domain. The door of Marjorie's "house" stood
open as though hospitably awaiting the arrival of
the guest. Its dainty pink and whiteness shed a
light and beauty, infinitely cheering on a dark day.

"And now to give you something to dress up in."
Loosing Veronica's hand, Marjorie crossed the
room and threw open the door of a large dress
closet. "Yours to command," she offered with a
hospitable gesture. Pressing a button in the wall
the wardrobe sprang alight, disclosing the finery of
girlhood in all its rainbow hues.

"Oh, you choose a garment for me to luxuriate
in," Ronny returned. "I don't know the whys and
wherefores of your clothes."

Marjorie peered thoughtfully at her array of
gowns and selected a half-fitted negligee of old-
rose silk. A moment's search in a cunningly con-

trived shoe cupboard at one side of the closet, and she held up quilted satin slippers to match.

"Thank you, hospitable one." Veronica was already clear of her dark blue bengaline frock and reaching for the silken comfort of the negligee. Her wet pumps soon removed, she donned the soft slippers and settled back in a willow rocker with a sigh of satisfaction. "I can't begin to tell you how comfortable I am," she said. "I had to change cars this morning before eight, and in the rain. All I had to console me was the thought that I would be in Sanford before noon. God-mother doesn't know I am east. I didn't write her because I was anxious to give her a surprise. I'll go to see her tomorrow. I wanted to come to you first. I never had much chance to be here when I was 'Miss Archer's servant.' "

Ronny's tones rippled with amused laughter. An answering smile rose to Marjorie's lips. Memory recalled the sedate, reserved girl she had known as Veronica Browning. She was now beginning to glimpse the real Ronny; brilliant, high-spirited, sure of herself, with the independence of those who have known the bitterness of poverty.

"You are so different, Ronny," she said. "I mean from last year. Once in a great while I used to see flashes of you as you are now. I remember the night you danced that wonderful butterfly num-

ber at the Campfire. You seemed happy and so
much more like a real girl than as I saw you in
school each day. You are like a butterfly who is
so glad to be free of the chrysalis."

"How nice in you to compare me to anything so
beautiful as a butterfly. I am glad to be free of the
part I played last year. I am not sorry I played it,
though. Is Mignon La Salle going to Hamilton
College?" she asked, with an abrupt change of subject. "I hope not. I think I can never forgive her
for the trouble she made you. I never minded in
the least the way she treated me."

"No; Mignon is going to Smith College. She is
all right now, Ronny," Marjorie earnestly assured.
"When she faced about last spring she truly meant
it."

"You deserve the credit for having hauled her
through," was Ronny's blunt opinion. "I never
would have had the patience. A good many times
last year I was tempted to tell you who I really
was. I did not care to have the other girls know,
and Jerry was so curious about me. I was afraid it
might make trouble for you if you knew and they
didn't. The Lookouts would have been likely to
ask you about me. Then, if I had pledged you to
secrecy, it would have meant your refusal to answer
any questions concerning me. This year——"

Veronica broke off in the old way which had

always been so baffling to Marjorie. For an instant
a vague sense of disappointment visited her. It was
as though Ronny had once again suddenly dropped
the curtain of mystery between them.

Her brown eyes fixed with unconscious solemnity on her guest, she became aware that Veronica
was laughing at her. "I know what you are thinking," Ronny declared. "You think I am the same
aggravating old mystery who used never to finish a
sentence. Good reason why I chopped off a remark
I was about to make. I almost told you a secret."
Her tone was now purposely tantalizing. "Had I
best tell you now or wait awhile?"

The entrance into the room of Mrs. Dean, bear-
ing a lacquered tray, on which was a steaming cup
of consommé and a plate of small crisp rolls, interrupted any confidence Ronny might have been on
the point of making. Lingering for a few minutes'
talk with Veronica, Mrs. Dean left the two girls
with the reminder that the luncheon bell would soon
ring.

Marjorie, meanwhile, had learned something new
of Ronny. She realized that now her friend was
only playing at secrecy. Ronny would never again
be a mystery to her as in the past.

"I've learned something about you, Ronny
Lynne," she commented in merry accusation. "You
love to tease. Well, you can't tease me. As for

your old secret you may do just as you please.
You may tell me now or after while. I'm not a
bit curious. Ahem! I won't say I am not *interested*. Wouldn't you like to tell me now?"

She laid a coaxing hand on Ronny's arm. The
latter's radiant face was an index to pleasant news.

"Would I? Perhaps." Ronny pretended to deliberate. "Well, listen hard. Once upon a time
there was a person named Ronny who decided to go
to college. She had heard about a college named
Hamilton, and——"

"You're going to Hamilton! You're going to
Hamilton!" Marjorie had sprung from her chair
and was performing a dance of jubilation about
Veronica. "It is the best old secret I ever heard!"

"I hoped you would be pleased." There were
tears just back of Ronny's eyes. She loved Marjorie with the great strength of a first friendship.
Naturally she was moved by the hearty reception
of her news.

"*Pleased!* That doesn't express it! This morning I was lonesome and wished something pleasant
would happen. The girls are all away from Sanford. Lucy Warner and I are the only Lookouts
at home. Lucy is secretary to Mr. Forbes, a Sanford lawyer, so I don't see her very often. I never
dreamed that the rain would bring me you. And
now comes the crowning happiness! You are

going to be with me at Hamilton. I think I am a very lucky Lookout." Marjorie had paused in front of Veronica, hands resting lightly on the arms of the latter's chair. "When you left Sanford last June, Ronny, had you any idea then of entering Hamilton?"

"No." Ronny shook a decided head. "I was not sure of coming east again for a long while. Father missed me dreadfully last year. I could tell that from his letters. I thought he would ask me to stay at home and engage a tutor for me. After I had been at home awhile we went on a pony riding trip over some of his fruit ranches. We had lots of long talks and I told him a great deal about you. He was much interested in the Lookouts and asked a good many questions about the club. He asked which college you expected to enter, and if I would like to go east again to college. I found that he really wished me to go to an eastern college, provided I was of the same mind. He always gives me the privilege of choice. Of course, I chose Hamilton. So here I am. I shall divide my visits between you and God-mother until time to go to Hamilton, and then we'll journey into the far country of college together along with as many of the Lookouts as shall decide for Hamilton."

"Jerry is going to be a Hamiltonite," returned Marjorie, her bright face showing her happiness.

"Muriel Harding, too. I am not sure about Lucy Warner, Ronny. She may have to wait until next year to enter college. She won't let anyone help her with her personal expenses."

"I expected some such hitch in her plans," was Ronny's almost grim reply." I would have offered her personal aid last June, but knew it would not be best then. I intended to write you about it. When I decided for college I knew I could talk things over with you and plan how to help Lucy while on this visit."

"If anyone can persuade her that she really ought to enter Hamilton, this year, it will be you," Marjorie asserted confidently.

"I will do my best," promised Ronny. "I ought to have made that scholarship cover everything in the way of expense down to a shoestring. I was positive Lucy would win it. She is so proud. I merely tried to save her dignity by offering the regulation scholarship."

The musical tinkle of a bell from below stairs announced luncheon. Marjorie caught Ronny's hands and drew her up from her chair.

"There's the luncheon bell," she announced. "Come along, Ronny. We have some glorious news to tell Captain."

Their arms twined about each other's waists, the two friends walked slowly toward the half open door. There they stopped to talk. A second and louder jingling of the bells soon informed them that they were loiterers.

"That's Captain," laughed Marjorie. "She knows we've stopped to talk. Delia rang the bell first time. She only tinkled it a little."

Accelerating their pace, the two gaily descended the stairs. More fully the joy of the occasion was borne upon Veronica. It was wonderful to her to be so near and dear to a girl like Marjorie. More, this happy state of affairs would continue all year. There would be no cloud of mystery betweeen them as had been at high school. She was determined also that no clouds should obscure Marjorie's college sky if she could prevent their gathering. If Marjorie's strict adherence to truth and justice brought her the disfavor of the unworthy, she would not have to contend against them single-handed.

CHAPTER IV

CONCERNING JEREMIAH.

Luncheon proved a merry little meal. When one has been suddenly lifted out of the dumps by the arrival of a friend from afar, and afterward doubly cheered by exceptionally good news, the dreariness of a rainy day is soon forgotten.

Returned to the living room after luncheon, Marjorie drew forward a deep, soft-cushioned chair with wide padded arms.

"Take this chair, Ronny," she invited. "It's the most comfortable old thing! In winter it is my pet lounging place at twilight. I love to curl up in it and watch the firelight. Captain likes that wicker chair near the table. General and I always fight over this one. If he gets it first, I try to tip him out of it. I might as well try to move a mountain. He braces his feet and sits and laughs at me. Ruffle, my big Angora cat, claims it, too. He always looks so injured if I lift him from it."

"An extremely popular chair," commented Ronny, smiling. Settling back in it, she added: "I don't wonder you all fight for it. I shall enter the lists, too."

"You are welcome to it. You're company. It's only the Deans who won't respect one another's claims, Captain excepted. By the Deans, I mean General, Ruffle and me."

"Much obliged for clearing me of the charge," her captain remarked with twinkling eyes. "You should hear those squabbles, Veronica. They are noisy enough to bring the house down."

Veronica laughed, yet into her gray eyes sprang

a wistful light. "My father loves to tease me like that," she said. "We had such good times this summer at Mañana. That is the name of our largest ranch. We live there most of the time."

"Mañana?" Marjorie looked questioningly at Ronny. "That means 'morning' in Spanish, doesn't it? I know a few Spanish words. General speaks the language. His trips often take him to Mexico."

"Yes, it also means 'tomorrow,'" Ronny answered. "The full name of our Mañana is 'Lucero de la Mañana.' It means 'Star of the Morning.' I named it. Father bought it when I was twelve years old. The first time I saw it was one morning before seven. We were on a riding trip and could look down on it from a height. It was so beautiful, I asked Father to find out if it were for sale. It belonged to a Spanish woman, Donna Dolores de Mendoza. She was willing to part with it, as she wished to go to Spain to live. So Father bought it. I hope someday you will visit me there. I shall never be satisfied until the Dean family are under the Lynnes' roof tree."

"Someday," Marjorie made hopeful promise. "General has said he would take us on a western trip sometime."

"I hope that 'sometime' will be next summer," returned Ronny. "When I grow to know your worthy General well, I shall interview him on the subject."

Veronica's allusion to her far western home furnished Marjorie with an opportunity she had long desired. She was anxious to hear more of Ronny's life prior to her advent into Sanford. She had, therefore, a great many interested questions to ask which she knew Ronny would now be willing to answer. Formerly, while Ronny had been securely wrapped in her cloak of reserve, Marjorie had never attempted to question her personally.

Ronny, in turn, had an equal number of questions to ask regarding Sanford and the Lookouts. The afternoon slipped away before either of the reunited friends was aware that it had gone.

"Do you suppose we'll ever catch up in talking?" Ronny asked in pretended despair, as the three women lingered over the dessert at dinner that evening.

"Oh, after a long while," easily assured Marjorie. "You see I couldn't get you to talk about yourself last year, so we lost a good deal of time. I am actually ashamed for asking you so many questions, Ronny. Still there were so many things I wanted to ask you last year and did not feel free to. Wait until you see Jerry. She will ask you more questions than I have. She said in her last letter to me that she had no news to tell. Well, I shall have some news to tell her when she comes home. She will be so surprised when she——"

"*Surprised?* Well, yes; *quite* a lot."

The familiar voice that gave utterance to this pithy affirmation proceeded from the doorway leading into the reception hall. It electrified the placid trio at the table. Three heads turned simultaneously at the sound. Marjorie made a dive for the doorway.

"Jeremiah!" she exclaimed, with a joyful rising inflection on the last syllable. "Wherever did you come from? This is my third splendid surprise today. You can see for yourself who's here. You've had one surprise, at least." Marjorie clung to Jerry with enthusiastic fervor.

"I have, I have," agreed Jerry, putting two plump arms around Ronny, who had come forward the instant she grasped the situation. "Now how in the world do you happen to be here, mysterious Mystery? You are the last person I thought would be on the job to welcome me to our city."

"How long have *you* been here? That is what I should like to know," Marjorie interposed, patting the hand she held between her own.

"Long enough to hear all you said about me. I'm simply furious. No; I am perfectly delighted, I mean. Now what do I mean?" Jerry showed her white even teeth in a genial grin.

"We didn't say anything about you that would either delight you or make you furious. I know you didn't hear a single thing we said, except maybe the last sentence. How did you get in? Not by the front door or we would have heard the bell. Now confess: Delia let you in by the back door." Marjorie waved a triumphant finger before Jerry's nose as she made this conjecture.

"I'll never tell how I came in. No; that won't do, Geraldine. You must try to be civil to these Deans. They may ask you to stay a few days and you——" Jerry paused significantly, then sidled up to Mrs. Dean. "I'm so pleasant to have around," she simpered. "You will positively adore me when you get used to my ways." She put both arms around Mrs. Dean and gave her a resounding kiss.

"You may stay as long as you please, and the longer you stay the better pleased we shall be." Her invitation thus extended, Mrs. Dean was now assisting Jerry to remove her long coat of tan covert cloth. "How did you manage to keep so dry, Jerry?" she inquired. "It has been raining steadily all evening. Veronica came to us thoroughly drenched."

"The beautiful truth is, Delia hung my coat in front of the range and dried it. I had an umbrella, too, and I ran like a hunter the minute I left the taxi. I made the driver stop at the corner below the house and I ducked in at the side gate. I landed on your back porch just as Delia was going to serve the dessert. I asked her not to tell you I was here. It's a great wonder she didn't laugh and give me away."

"I noticed she had a broad smile on her face when she came into the dining room. I thought it was in honor of Ronny. Here she was aiding and abetting *you,* Jeremiah Macy! She knows I have been anxiously waiting for you to come home. Just wait till I see her!"

Marjorie chuckled in anticipation of her interview with Delia. The latter would regard Jerry's stealthy arrival as a huge joke in which she had played an important part.

"I thought a relative had come to see you," Jerry continued. "Delia said it was a young lady from away off. That's all she seemed to want to tell me. I didn't quiz her. It was none of my business."

"That is the time Delia fooled you," Ronny asserted. "Delia knows me. She wanted to surprise you, too."

"All right for Delia. Wait until *I* interview her for keeping so quiet about you." All of which pointed to a lively session for Delia. "Anyhow I had some cherry pudding with whipped cream. I saw it the minute I struck the kitchen. I hoped it wouldn't give out before it got around to me.

There was enough, though, for Delia and me. We emptied the dish."

"All this going on behind my back!" Mrs. Dean made an unsuccessful effort to look highly displeased. "I shall have to discipline the commissary department for smuggling vagrants into the house under my very nose. Not to mention distributing pudding with a free hand!"

"Vagrants! She means me." Jerry rolled her eyes as though greatly alarmed. "I see I'll have to swallow the insult. If I make a fuss I may be put out."

"Promise good conduct in future and we'll try to overlook the past," Marjorie graciously conceded.

"Thank you, kind lady! I wasn't always like this. Once I had a home——". Jerry gave vent to a loud snivel. "I lost it. Now all I can say is:

"Into your house some tramps must fall,
    Some Deans must be made aweary."

Sobbing out this pathetic sentiment, Jerry endeavored to lean on Marjorie, with disastrous results. They were saved from toppling over by landing with force against Veronica.

"Here, here!" expostulated Ronny. Don't add assault and battery to vagrancy. Have some respect for me. I'm a real guest. I arrived by the front door."

"Excuse me and blame Marjorie for being an unstable prop. Try to regard me as your friend." Jerry leered confidently at Ronny.

"I'll think it over. You are the funniest old goose ever. I'll try to prevail upon the Deans to let you stay."

"Oh, I think I can manage them," Jerry returned in a confident stage whisper.

"Yes, we are going to be kind to our tramp now." Marjorie gently propelled Jerry to the table and shoved her, unresisting, into a chair. "You had dessert. Now you had better have the rest of the dinner. While Delia is getting it ready you can tell us how it all happened. How did you get away from the beach before your folks were ready to come home?"

"I teased Mother good and hard and she finally said 'yes.' It took me about two hours to pack and wish the beach good-bye. The folks will be home Saturday. I'll have three whole days with you girls. I hadn't figured on the distinguished presence of Miss Veronica Browning Lynne."

"Neither had I," smiled Marjorie. "The best part of Ronny's visit is that it is going to last until the very day I start for Hamilton. Ronny is going to Hamilton, too, Jerry."

"Did I get that right?" Jerry placed an assisting hand to one ear. Say it again, will you? Hooray!" Jerry picked up a dessert fork and waved it jubilantly. "The three of us; and Muriel Harding as a fourth staunch supporter! We can teach the Hamilton faculty how to act and revolutionize the whole college. Oh, yes! Lucy Warner makes a fifth. Ummm! She will have to be supported until she gets on her ear. Then she'll freeze solid and support herself."

Neither Ronny nor Marjorie could refrain from laughing at this view of Lucy. It was so precisely like her.

"Thank goodness there won't be Mignon to reform." Jerry sighed exaggerated relief. "Any more sieges like the four years' siege of Mignon ahead of me, and I'd stay at home and go to night school for a change. Talk about the wars of the Trojans! They were simple little scraps compared with the rows we've had at Sanford High with various vandals."

Delia appearing from the kitchen with a heavily laden tray, the three girls greeted her with a concerted shout. Not in the least dismayed, she only beamed more broadly, as each of the trio attempted to take her to task, and refused to commit herself.

After Jerry had made a substantial repast, she

was triumphatnly conducted to her room by Ronny and Marjorie.

"Have you a kimono or negligee in your bag, Jerry? If you have, put it on and be comfy. If you haven't, speak now and you can have one of mine. Captain will be on guard duty in the living room this evening. If any one calls they won't have the pleasure of seeing us. We are going to have an old-time talking bee in my house. Come along as soon as you are ready."

"I have a kimono in my traveling bag. It has probably acquired about a thousand wrinkles by this time," returned Jerry. "Wrinkled or no, I shall hail it with joy. You may expect me at your house in about fifteen minutes."

"All right," Marjorie called over her shoulder, as she and Ronny left Jerry. "Don't be longer than that. Remember we have weighty matters to discuss this evening. If we began early enough we may have the affairs of the universe settled before midnight."

When within the prescribed fifteen minutes Jerry joined her chums, it was their own personal affairs that came up for discussion. Enough had happened during the summer in their own little sphere to keep them talking uninterruptedly all evening.

"There is one thing we must do before we leave Sanford for college and that is pass the Lookout

Club on to the senior class at Sanford High. You know we planned to do so when we organized the club, Jeremiah," Marjorie reminded.

"That's so," Jerry agreed, "but how do we go about it? If we just hand it to the senior class, they may not carry it on as we would wish them to. It was really our own little private club. I'm not crazy to continue it as a sorority."

"We ought to, Jerry, just the same. The Lookouts have been a credit to Sanford High, and the influence we have tried to exert should be carried on each year by fifteen seniors." Marjorie spoke with conviction. "I have thought a good deal about it this summer. I believe the best way for us to do is for each of the Lookouts to propose the name of one member of the present senior class. As soon as the other girls come home we will have a meeting. The names of the candidates can be written on slips of paper and read out to the club in turn. If any one of us objects to another's choice, she must say so and state her reason. If it is sufficient, the name will be dropped and the Lookout who proposed it may propose another."

"That's a good idea. While we can be trusted, I hope not to pick lemons, slackers and shirkers, still it makes our choice surer to have it approved by the gang. So long as we are to be the ones to do the choosing, I begin to see light." Jerry had begun to show more enthusiasm.

"It's really organizing what one might call a new Lookout chapter. We are the charter members and will continue to run our chapter as we like. Next year the girls we choose will select their fifteen members for a new chapter, and so on, indefinitely," said Veronica.

"We need these new girls, Jerry," Marjorie earnestly pointed out. "We can't look after the day nursery and go to college, too. While we have hired help there, and Miss Allison, you know, is always ready to do all she can to help keep it running smoothly, we need the personal influence of the seniors at the nursery. There should be two club members to take their turn each day from four to six, as we did."

"Who has been looking after that part of it this summer?" Jerry demanded abruptly, her keen eyes on Marjorie. "I wrote and asked you that and you never answered my question. You are the one who has probably been making a slave of yourself at that same nursery while the rest of us have been having a lovely time."

"I have been down there twice a week from four to six," Marjorie replied. "Sometimes Captain went with me. Thanks to *that* generous person," she indicated Ronny, "we could afford to engage some one to amuse the children. Ronny put five hundred dollars in bank for a vacation fund and never said a single word about it. When she was half way to California I received a note from Mr. Wendell asking me to call at the bank. You can imagine what a surprise it was to me. It was fine in you to think of it, Ronny. The girls were worried, for we found out that all of the Lookouts except me, were going to be away from Sanford at about the same time.

"While we had quite a good deal of money in the treasury we didn't think of engaging anyone from outside," she continued. "It worked beautifully. Miss Stratton, a kindergarten teacher, needed the work on account of having an invalid sister to support. Then, Nellie Wilkins, one of the mill girls, had been sick for a long time and when she was well enough to go back to her work as a weaver there was no position for her. She is a very sweet girl and knows all the children. She was a great help to Miss Stratton and I would like her to have the position permanently at the nursery. She knows all the songs and games now that Miss Stratton taught the children and is the best person one could have there."

"Whew!" whistled Jerry. "Things have certainly been happening at the nursery." You are simply splendid, Ronny. You are always thinking

of some way to help people.   Just wait until I take
my presidential chair as chief boss of the Lookouts.
I will publish your noble deed abroad."

"If you *don't,* I *will,*" emphasized Marjorie.
"There isn't much we can say to tell you how grateful we are to you, Ronny."

"Don't say anything."   A bright flush had risen
to Ronny's cheeks.   "I knew the girls would be
away.   I thought you would be quite apt to worry
about the nursery and spend a lot of time there for
conscientious reasons.   I was thinking more of you
I presume than the nursery."

"It was a great relief," Marjorie made honest
response.   "Besides, it helped two splendid girls
along."

"Then let it rest at that.   Never mind about pub-
lishing my, thus-called, noble deed at a club meeting.   I prefer not to let my right hand know what
my left happens to be doing," declared Ronny.
What we must think of is getting the new Lookout
chapter started.   We ought to have it organized
by the fifth of September so it will stand on its own
feet.   After the fifth you know what a rush there
will be.   We shall be going to farewell teas, lunch-
eons and parties.   At least I hope so.   Last year I
had very good times.   This fall things have changed.
Now I'd love to dance and be happy with the crowd
of Sanford boys and girls who were so friendly

with me when I was a senior. Marjorie said today,
Jerry, that I was like a butterfly that had won free
of the chrysallis. The butterfly is anxious to spread
its wings for a few last delightful flights around
Sanford."

CHAPTER V.

THE BREAKING UP OF THE OLD GUARD.

"THIS saying good-bye business is growing har-
rowing," complained Jerry one hazy September
morning. She stood with her chums on the station
platform, waving farewell to Florence Johnston,
who was leaving for Markham College, a western
university. "This is the third time for us at the
station this week. Monday it was Mignon, Daisy
Griggs and Gertrude Aldine, all bound for Smith.
Wednesday it was Esther, Rita, Susan and Irma.
I am not over the blues yet on account of losing
Susan and Irma. I wish they had chosen Hamilton instead of Wellesley."

The seven Lookouts still left in Sanford were
strolling soberly across the green station yard to the
drive behind the station where Jerry had parked the
Macys' ample touring car. She had elected to drive
it that morning because of its capacity.

"Harriet and I are going to be the lonesome ones before long," remarked Constance Stevens, her blue eyes roving somberly from friend to friend. The private conservatory Constance and Harriet were to enter did not open until the latter part of October. This would make them the last to leave Sanford. "It is going to seem awfully queer for us without you girls, isn't it, Harriet?"

"Yes." Harriet was looking unduly solemn. "Still we knew long ago that it would have to come sometime; this breaking up of the old crowd."

"We must try to be together a lot during vacations. Most of us will be home for Thanksgiving, and all of us for Christmas and Easter," was Marjorie's philosophical consolation.

"Well, we're going to have one last good old frolic at Connie's tonight, anyway," was Jerry's cheering reminder.

"I can't come tonight, Constance," Lucy Warner announced in her brusque fashion. "I must give these last few evenings to Mother. Besides, I don't feel at home in your crowd when the boys are there. I don't care much about young men. I never know what to say to them," she added, coloring slightly.

"I understand the way you feel about it," Constance returned with a smile. She had once been visited by the same discomfiture in the first days of her friendship with Marjorie. The others were laughing at Lucy's blunt avowal. "I'll forgive you for turning down my party. You know we would love to have you with us, but if you were not at ease it would be hard for you."

"Yes, it would. Much obliged." Lucy's terse agreement provoked fresh laughter.

Ronny had promised Marjorie to take Lucy in hand and try to overcome her objections to entering Hamilton College that fall. Three times she besieged Lucy before success came. On the third interview, Ronny learned the real difficulty. Very solemnly Lucy told her the story of the Observer and her subsequent ingratitude toward Marjorie. Ronny had felt righteous anger flame within her as she had listened. She had almost wished she had never offered a scholarship in behalf of such an ingrate. Her brain clearing of its hasty resentment, she had been visited by the same divine pity for poor, embittered Lucy that had swayed Marjorie on the occasion of the 'Observer confession.

Very cleverly Ronny had seized upon the confession to move Lucy from her torturing resolve. She argued that, as it was Marjorie's wish to see Lucy enter college with herself and friends, she therefore owed it to Marjorie as an amend honorable. Her point gained, Ronny managed also to persuade Lucy to accept financial help from her if necessary. This she reluctantly promised to do, provided she were allowed to repay her young benefactor when in position to do so. Thus Lucy became the fifth Lookout, Hamilton-bound, greatly to Marjorie's delight.

"What you ought to do is practice hanging around with our gang until you are not the least bit scared at Hal or Laurie or the rest of our boys," Jerry advised. "They aren't ogres and hob-goblins. There is really nothing very awe-inspiring about a young man. If you had lived in the same house with Hal as long as I have, you would know how to talk to him all right enough."

"I haven't; therefore I don't," Lucy returned concisely, but with an open good nature which showed how greatly she had emerged from her shell since becoming a Lookout.

"There goes Flora Frisbee," suddenly called out Muriel, as she exchanged a gay salute with a girl who had just passed in an automobile.

"Where?" inquired three or four voices. A particularly well liked senior, Flora had acquired a further high standing with the Lookouts as the president of the new chapter.

"Too late. She is out of sight. I just happened to see her as she flashed by in her brother's roadster. I think she is going to make a dandy president. Don't you?"

"The very best." It was Jerry who answered

"I am certainly glad the new chapter is going so nicely. They have settled down to that nursery detail like veterans."

"I was so proud of them that day at Muriel's when we organized the new chapter," praised Ronny.

"They did as well as we when we began," commented Muriel. "If only they keep it up. We picked the best of the seniors."

Following a meeting at Jerry's home, at which the Lookouts had selected the candidates for the new chapter, a second meeting had been held at Muriel's. Each charter Lookout had gallantly escorted her choice there. Fifteen gratified seniors had listened to the rules of the club and promised to live up to them. They had pledged themselves to faithfully carry on the work of their absent elder sisters at the day nursery and be always ready to help those in need of friendly aid. They had then capably taken up the pleasant task of electing their officers and performed it with business-like snap.

Soon after their organization they had accompanied the charter members to the nursery and spent a merry afternoon getting acquainted with the little ones. From then on they had begun their regular duty tours accompanied, at first, by one of the old guard on each tour. Soon accustoming themselves to the routine, their elder sisters breathed more freely and set about attending to their own manifold affairs.

"We hope we picked fifteen winners. If we didn't we'll soon know it with a bang. That nursery will run on wheels, minus one trouble maker. Just one will throw the whole concern up in the air. While I don't doubt our new sisters, let time do its perfect work. So says Jeremiah. She says further, get into the car all of you. I'm going to take you straight home. I'm going to a party tonight and I have no time to waste standing talking on the corner. There will be young men at that party!" Jerry dropped her voice to a hoarse melodramatic whisper and stared wildly at Lucy, chin thrust forward.

"I can't help that. I—I should worry. I'm no buttinski." Lucy's unexpected use of slang raised a gale of laughter.

"I am afraid you learned that from me. You are growing up precautious. You need a guardian." With this Jerry bundled Lucy into the tonneau of the machine and turned her over to Marjorie and Muriel who had already climbed into the car.

In her usual energetic fashion she proceeded to drive her chums to their various homes, where she dropped them with scant ceremony. "I know you are all in a hurry to get home," she sweetly assured them. "If you aren't, I am. It's all one. Good-bye. Shall I see you this evening? You had better believe it."

The informal gathering at Gray Gables would comprise the remaining Lookouts of the charter and six or seven of the Sanford boys whom Constance knew best and who were intimate friends of Laurie Armitage's. Marjorie, in particular, was happy in the invitation. She thought it so beautiful that Connie, who had known the bitterest want, should be the hostess at their last frolic, commemorative of their high school days.

As she dressed for the party that evening, her thoughts traveled back to the eventful night of the freshman dance when Constance had worn the blue gown and made her entrance into the social side of high school under difficulties. At that time she had been a very humble person. Now she was perhaps the most admired young woman in Sanford on account of her beautiful voice. Things had changed a good deal in four years for Connie, Marjorie reflected. She took a special pride in her appearance that night, not only in honor of Constance, but because she owed it to herself to look her best on that last happy evening with her friends.

When Veronica entered Marjorie's house, attired in her white lace Commencement Day frock, a pale blue evening cape composed of many ruffles of chiffon hanging over one arm, she found a pensive little figure in white occupying the pink and white window seat. Marjorie was also wearing her graduation gown and looking utterly lovely in it.

"I'm mooning," she announced, turning her curly head as Ronny entered, her eyes very bright. "It's a perfect night, Ronny. Almost warm enough to go without a wrap. Hal will be here for us. I forgot to tell you. He called me on the 'phone yesterday to ask me if he might take us over in his car."

Veronica smiled slightly at this frank announcement. It contained not a trace of self-consciousness. Long ago Ronny had glimpsed Hal Macy's mind regarding Marjorie. She knew the latter to be the likable young man's ideal and had seen boyish worship of Marjorie more than once in his clear blue eyes. She also understood that Marjorie was wholly fancy free. While she valued Hal as a near friend, any awakening to a deeper sentiment on her part belonged to a far distant day.

CHAPTER VI.

THE BOWKNOT OF AFFECTION.

THAT evening as Hal assisted the two girls into the tonneau of the limousine, he was of the romantic opinion that he had merely persuaded a couple of stray moonbeams to ride with him. The light of the fair, increasing moon endowed the duo with a peculiar ethereal beauty which gave him a feeling of reverence. Girls were mostly like flowers was his boyish comparison. The most beautiful flower of them all was Marjorie. Someday he would dare tell her so, but not for a long time.

Arrived at Gray Gables Hal had no further opportunity to "moon." The rest of the company had arrived and were impatiently awaiting them. The limousine had hardly come to a stop on the drive when out of the house they trooped, shouting the Sanford and Weston High School yells by way of welcome. Danny Seabrooke and the Crane then broke into the "Stars and Stripes" on mouth organs. Miles Burton rattled out a lively accompaniment on little Charlie Stevens' toy drum.

"I had no idea I was so popular." Hal bowed his thanks to the noisy musicians.

"You are not," the Crane hastened to inform him. "That choice selection we just rendered was in honor of the girls. Don't credit yourself with everything. It's horribly conceited."

"I'm glad you named it as a 'selection,' Hal made scathing retort.

"What, may I ask, would you name it?" queried Danny with a dangerous affability.

"Making night hideous, or, a disgraceful racket, or, the last convulsions of a would-be jazz band. Any little appellation like that would be strictly appropriate." Hal beamed ironically on the three. "Nice little drummer boy you have there."

Supposedly offended, Danny could not repress a loud snicker at this fling. Miles Burton stood six feet, minus shoes. With Charlie's toy drum strung round his neck on a narrow blue ribbon, he was distinctly mirth-inspiring.

"Throw any more remarks like that about me and you'll find out my real disposition," warned Miles in a deep bass growl.

"Come ladies; let us hasten on before trouble overtakes us—me, I mean. Back, varlets. Grab your instruments of torture and begone." Hal grandly motioned the objectionable varlets out of the way.

"That's what I say," called Jerry from the top step. For once I agree with Hal. Let the girls come up on the porch, can't you? You four sillies can stay outside and rave. Notice how well Laurie and Harry are behaving. Try to be a little like them, if you can."

"You can't know them as I do," rumbled Miles.

"No; I *guess not*," emphasized Hal. "Well, I'd rather be called a silly than a varlet."

"That will do from all of you." Jerry ran down the steps and with a few energetic waves of the arms drove the masculine half of the guests up onto the brightly-lighted veranda. There the entire company lingered to talk, presently strolling into the long old-fashioned drawing room which Constance used for dancing purposes when entertaining her friends.

"Be happy and make yourselves at home," she said in her pretty, graceful fashion. "Father and Uncle John will soon be here to play for us. They are helping Mr. Beaver, the leader of the Sanford orchestra, organize some of the Sanford working boys into an orchestra. It's a fine idea. I think Father and Uncle John will help him all they can whenever they are at home."

Marjorie cast a quick, inquiring look toward Constance. Her eyes luminous with affection, she asked: "Has it come at last, Connie?"

"Yes, Marjorie," Constance answered, in a proud, happy tone. "I wuld like you to know," she continued, turning to the others, "that Uncle John is to be a first violin in Father's symphony orchestra. You can understand just how glad we feel about it."

Connie's news met with an echoing shout. All present cherished the warmest regard for gentle Uncle John, who had ever been so willing to play for them. Far removed from poverty, he had gradually regained the lost faculty of memory and could now be relied upon for symphony work.

"Oh, just wait until he gets home!" promised Hal. "Won't he get a reception, though?"

"Surest thing in the world!" Laurie's dark blue eyes were darker from emotion. Laurie had known for a very long time that, if Constance's adopted family were not his own, some future day, it would not be his fault.

"That explains why we haven't seen Charlie," smiled Marjorie. "He is actually helping, at last, to organize a big band. I meant to ask for him. There was so much sarcasm being hurled back and forth, my voice would have been lost in the uproar," she slyly added.

"He took his violin and music. The music was a lot of old stray song sheets. He will play them

and put everyone out, if he has a chance," Constance predicted with an infectious little giggle.

The entrance of Miss Allison into the drawing
room brought the young folks to their feet. Her
fondness for youth made her a welcome addition at
their parties. She particularly enjoyed Danny Seabrooke's antics and the sham penalties they invariably brought on him.

"You young gentlemen will soon be leaving for
college as well as our girls," she remarked to Hal.
"I am glad Laurie has decided to go through college before making music his profession. He really
needs the college training. Constance, on the contrary, will do as well to begin her training for
grand opera at once. She must study Italian and
Spanish. That, with her vocal practice, will keep
her fully occupied. How I shall miss my boys and
girls! They have been life to me." Miss Allison's
delicate features saddened unconsciously.

A muffled sob, too realistic to be genuine, rent the
air at her right. Her sad expression vanished as
her eyes lighted upon the mourner. Slumped into
the depths of a big velvet chair, Danny was struggling visibly with his sorrowful emotions.

"To see us all here tonight, who would dream
of the parting to come so soon-n; s-o s-o-o-o-on-n!"
he wailed, covering his freckled, grief-stricken countenance with both hands. No one arising to as-

suage his sorrow, his gurgles and sobs grew louder.

"Won't some one please choke off that bellow?" Laurie viewed the perpetrator of the melancholy sounds with a cold, unrelenting eye.

"*De*-lighted." Hal rose from a seat on the davenport beside Marjorie and advanced with threatening deliberation upon Danny.

"You needn't mind. I am getting used to the idea of parting now." The "bellow" ceased like magic. Danny spoke in a small, sad voice that might have belonged to a five-year-old girl. "Soon I shall be able to contemplate it without a single tear. I could part from *you*," he suddenly recovered his own voice, "or that ruffian of an Armitage, and smile; yes, sir; actually *smile*. I'd rather part at any time, and from anybody than to be murderously 'choked off' by you two bullies."

Danny hastily arose, after this defiant declaration, and retreated to the lower end of the room. Crowding himself into a small rocking chair belonging to Charlie, he rocked and smirked at Hal, who had followed him to the chair and now stood over him.

"Move back a trifle, Mr. Macy. I refuse to be responsible for other people's shins. I have all I can do to take care of my own. If I were to kick you, *accidently*, I should be *so* sorry!"

"Oh, undoubtedly! Wouldn't you, though?"

Bending, with one swift movement of the arm, Hal upset the rocker and its grinning occupant. "Now will you be good?" he inquired sarcastically. Leaving the struggling wag to right himself, Hal strolled back to Marjorie.

The room rang with laughter at Danny's upheaval, nor did it lessen as he went through a series of ridiculous attempts to rise from the floor. In the midst of the fun Charlie Stevens marched into the drawing room, his little leather violin case tucked importantly under one arm, his music under the other. Behind him were Mr. Stevens and John Roland.

"What for is he doing to my chair?" Charlie asked very severely.

"He's trying to part with it, Charlie, and he's either stuck in it or pretending he is," Harry Lenox replied to the youngster.

"You mustn't ever sit in a chair that don't look like you, Danny," reproved Charlie. "That chair looks like me. You ought to know better."

This was too much for the erring Daniel. With a shout of mirth he slipped free of the chair, and, catching up the little boy, swung him to his shoulder. "You're the funniest little old kid on creation!" he exclaimed.

"That's what I think," returned Charlie, with an innocent complacency that again brought down the

house. From that on Charlie divided honors with
Uncle John, who was due to receive the sincere congratulations of the young folks he had so often
made happy by his music. To see the white-haired,
patient-faced old musician surrounded by his young
friends was a sight that Miss Allison never forgot.
When, a little later, she led Charlie from the room,
bedward bound, there was thankfulness in her heart
because she had found the lonely people of the
Little Gray House in time.

With the musicians on the scene, dancing was
promptly begun and continued unflaggingly until a
late supper was served in the dining room. There
a surprise awaited Marjorie. While the company
were engaged in eating the dessert, she had a dim
idea that something unusual was pending. She dis-
missed it immediately as a vague fancy.

Next she became aware that a silence had settled
down upon the supper party. Then Hal Macy rose
from his chair and said in his clear, direct tones:
"I am going to read you a little tribute to a very
good friend of ours. I know you will agree with
me that Marjorie Dean is largely responsible for a
great many pleasant times we have enjoyed since
we have known her. By that I mean, not only the
merry evenings we have spent at her home, but the
happiness that has been ours because of her fine
influence. As well as I could, for I am no poet,

I have tried to put our sentiments into verse.
While the meter may be faulty, the inspiration is
flawless."

Applause greeted this frank, graceful little pre-
amble. When it had subsided, Hal read his verses.
They fitly expressed, to the amazed, and all but
overcome, subject of them, the strength of her
friends' devotion. When he had finished she had
no words with which to reply. She was grateful
for the fresh round of approbation that began. It
gave her time to force back her tears. She did not
wish to break down if she could help it. She felt
that she owed it to Hal to thank him with a smile.

Hardly had quiet been restored when Constance
took the floor. In her right hand she held an
oblong box of white velvet. When she began to
speak, it was directly to Marjorie.

"What Hal has said to you, tonight, Marjorie,
is so true and beautiful that I couldn't better it if I
tried. He has expressed just the way we feel about
you, and what your sunny, dear influence has been
to us. We are afraid that someday you may run
away and leave us, so we wish to tie you to us with
a bowknot of affection."

Constance flitted the length of the table and
around the end to the side opposite from her seat.
Pausing behind Marjorie's chair, she slid a bare

white arm over her chum's shoulder and gently dropped the velvet box in front of her.

"I—I think I am going to cry," quavered Marjorie, "and I don't—want—to. Please—I—don't think— I —deserve———"

"I would advise you not to weep, Marjorie, or you may be treated as I was," warned Danny's bland tones. "It's not safe to sob around here."

Marjorie gave a half tremulous giggle that was the forerunner of recovery. Her tears checked, her hands trembled as she opened the white velvet box. Then her emotion became that of sheer wonder. Resting on its satin bed gleamed a string of graduated pearls from which hung a pearl pendant in the form of a bowknot.

"What made you do this?" she faltered. "It isn't *I* who have ever done anything to make you happy. It's *you* who have done everything to make me happy. I don't know what to say, only you are all so dear to me and thank you."

Constance standing beside Marjorie, an arm over her shoulder, Marjorie turned and childishly hid her flushed face in the frills of Connie's white organdie gown. While her thoughts were far from collected, she was experiencing a gladness of spirit because Constance could thus be her refuge at a time of overwhelming happiness.

CHAPTER VII.

ON THE THRESHOLD.

THE day after Constance's party brought Marjorie her General. With her father at home, after a lengthy absence, the sorrow of leaving her dear ones came forward again. Marjorie tried earnestly to keep all locked within and succeeded in a measure. Her general was not blind to the situation, however, and exerted himself on all occasions to keep his somewhat sober-faced lieutenant in good spirits.

On the morning of the day before Marjorie's departure for college, he announced his firm intention to help her pack. Nor did he swerve for an instant from his self-imposed duty. Breakfast over, he chased the lieutenant, screaming with laughter, up the stairs, landing in the middle of her "house" with a flying leap which an acrobat might have envied.

Regardless of his giggling daughter's ideas on the subject of packing, he swept down upon whatever lay nearest at hand and stowed it into one of the two open trunks. His efforts at being helpful were brief. Three determined pairs of hands intercepted his bold attempt to safely caché a small tab-oret, a large embroidered doyley, a satin chair cushion, a cut glass scent bottle and a Japanese vase. The energetic general's services were summarily dispensed with. He was banished from the room and the door shut in his face with a bang. In less than fifteen minutes he announced his return by a tatoo which threatened demolishment to the door. He was not re-admitted until he had given his word not to meddle with the packing. When Marjorie cautiously opened the door to him she found him staggering under a load of pasteboard boxes. He dumped them at her feet with a bow so profound that he all but stood on his head.

"There you are, unfeeling child!" he exclaimed. "How shocking to have a daughter who doesn't scruple to turn her poor old father out of her house!"

"Well, I let you into my house again, didn't I? Just please recall why you were turned out." Marjorie clasped both arms about her father's neck and swung on him gleefully. No one could be the least bit sad when General elected to be funny. Mrs. Dean and Ronny had already busied themselves with straightening the pile of boxes which had scattered when dumped to the floor.

"It's a good thing for you that you did," retorted Mr. Dean significantly. I might have gone away from the door and never NEVER have come back again. Then think what you would have missed."

"Oh, you would have had to come back sometime," was the serene assurance, as Marjorie plumped down on the floor to explore her newly-acquired riches.

They were all the heart of a girl could wish. One box contained a white chiffon evening scarf, thickly embroidered with tiny pink daisies. It draped itself in graceful folds to the waist, the ends reaching to the hem of her gown. Another held a white velour sports coat, the cut and design of it being particularly smart. From another box tumbled a dozen pairs of kid gloves. There was also a box of silk hosiery, another of fine linen handkerchiefs with butterfly and bowknot corners, her favorite designs, a box of engraved monogrammed stationery, and a pair of black satin evening slippers.

One long wide box she had left until the last. The lid removed and the folds of white tissue paper lifted, Marjorie breathed a little "Oh!" She stared in admiration at an exquisite evening frock of delicately shaded Chinese crêpe. It might have represented a spring dawn, shading as it did from creamy white to pale, indeterminate violet, and from violet to faintest pink. It was fashioned with a cunning simplicity of design which made it of the mode, yet strikingly individual. About the hem of the skirt, around the square neck and short sleeves and on the ends of the separate sash trailed shadowy clusters of violets, stamped upon the crêpe with an art known only to the Chinese.

"Where did you find it, General?" she gasped, as she held up the lovely, shimmering frock for her captain and Ronny to see. "I never expected to own a dream gown like this."

"It is a spring poem in shades," declared Ronny, lightly touching an end of the sash. "I can guess where it came from. Only a high-grade Chinese bazaar could furnish a gown of its kind. There are a few such shops west of the Mississippi. I never saw a gown so beautiful as this one even in San Francisco."

"It did not come from a shop. A Chinese merchant sent to China for it as a gift to Marjorie. In Denver I have a good friend, Mah Waeo, the last of an ancient Chinese house. He looks like an Eastern nobleman in carved ivory. He is a fine elderly man of irreproachable business and social reputation. He is a tea merchant and has great wealth. He lives very simply and spends most of his business gains in trying to educate and uplift his own people. We have been fast friends for fifteen years."

"I am familiar with that type of Chinese," Ronny spoke eagerly. "At home, Father and I have a good Chinese friend, too; Sieguf Tah. He lives alone on the smallest of his fruit ranches and acts as a benevolent father to all the China boys around there. The China boys, as they like to be called, are faithful, wise, intelligent and industrious. Best of all, they are strictly honest."

"I hope Mah Waeo will sometime make us a visit. I suppose you must have often invited him, General. He was a perfect dear to take such pains for a present for me." Marjorie raised a radiant face to her father. "All this is about the nicest surprise you ever gave me. I can't help liking my spring poem gown best of all. I shall write to Mah Waeo and tell him so and ask him myself to please make us a visit someday."

"I don't see how we are going to pack all these new treasures in your two trunks," Mrs. Dean practically interposed. "We shall have to do some skilful managing."

"They simply all *must* go," decreed Marjorie. I couldn't leave one behind.

"Which reminds me that I have something for you and Captain which I brought from the Golden West and have been saving until an appropriate moment. With your gracious permission, I will retire and return anon, as the old-style novelists loved to write."

Attired in a full, half-fitted morning gown of soft white silk, Ronny spread her arms, bowed down to the floor, East Indian fashion, and made a quick backward exit from the room.

"I am going to make Ronny dance for us tonight," planned Marjorie. She isn't going to pack that frock she has on. It will be a perfect dancing costume. We will have a little home party tonight; just the four of us. No; five. I want Delia to be with us, too. I've grown up under Delia's wing. She has always worked so hard to do her best for me whenever I have had a party, and she's been so good to me in all ways."

"By all means let us have Delia at our party," heartily indorsed Mr. Dean. "I shall ask her to dance the minuet with me. Do you think there will be music? I hope some one will be able to play a minuet fit to be heard. Did I hear you say that you had practised occasionally this summer?"

"No, you didn't, you old tease!" Marjorie sprang to her feet and made a rush at her general.

"Careful! I'm very fragile," he protested. Then he caught her in his strong arms and held her close. Her face buried against his shoulder, Marjorie knew that her father had loosed one arm from around her and drawn Captain into the circle of it.

Thus Veronica found them when she returned with her love offerings. She halted in the doorway, her face alight with tenderness for these three who had succeeded more nearly than any other persons she had ever known in living the ideal family life.

In her hand Ronny held two small black leather cases. The one contained a ring of pure gold, artistically chased with a running vine, and set with one large, perfect sapphire. This was intended for Marjorie. For Mrs. Dean she had bought a gold and pearl pin of ancient Peruvian handiwork. Both pieces of jewelry were from an old Spanish collection. She had bought them at a private sale in San Leandro for her friends and now delighted to add her tribute to Marjorie's happiness.

Standing very still in the doorway, her eyes meditatively sought the cases in her hand. Then she turned and stole noiselessy away from the little scene of adoration. Ronny knew that Marjorie was taking her real farewell of her general and captain.

CHAPTER VIII.

THE FIVE TRAVELERS.

"HAMILTON, did you say? Lead me to it." Jerry Macy opened her eyes and peered through the car window with revived interest. For an hour or

more she had been leaning back against the high
green plush car seat dozing lightly.   It was now
five o'clock in the afternoon and active Jerry was
feeling the strain of sitting still, hour after hour.

"No; I didn't say Hamilton." Muriel gently
tweaked Jerry's ear. "Wake up, sleepy head. That
station we just passed was Harcourt Hill. What
comes next? Muriel opened a time table and frown-
ingly perused it. It's hard to remember the names
of these little stations. Now where was I at? Oh,
yes; Harcourt Hill. Next comes Palmer; then
Tresholme. After that, West Hamilton, and then
Hamilton. Hamilton is the first stop this express
makes, thank goodness!"

"Muriel, you have really been invaluable to us on
this journey. Allow me to decorate you."   Ronny
leaned forward and pinned a huge lace-paper rosette
on the obliging Lookout. "Wear this for my sake."

While Muriel had been industriously engaged in
calling out the stations, Ronny had hastily ripped a
piece of decorative lace-paper from a half emptied
box of candied fruit, which the travelers had shared,
and busied herself with it. The result of her effort
she now generously tendered Muriel.

"I will—not." Muriel intercepted the rosette
before it found a place on the lapel of her brown
taffeta traveling coat and crumpled it in her hand.
"No such decorations for me when I'm so near

Hamilton. Suppose I forgot about it and wore it off the train. Some college wag would be sure to see it and post me in the grind book. Freshmen are good material for grinds. Remember that and keep your old rosettes out of sight."

"What would be written about you?" asked Lucy Warner curiously. "I can't see anything in that to write about."

"Don't think for a minute that enough couldn't be found in one foolish old paper rosette to make me feel silly for a half term, at least. I don't know what the method of teasing me would be. I do know that I am not going to give strange students a chance to try it."

"Then I shall hardly dare answer anyone, even if I am first addressed." Lucy fixed her green eyes on Muriel with an expression of alarm.

Muriel burst out laughing as she met the steady stare. She had never taken prim Lucy seriously. Lucy's austere solemnity always had an hilarious effect on keen-witted Muriel. Coupled with a direct stare from those peculiar greenish eyes, Muriel invariably felt a strong desire to laugh when in her presence. As a result, there was no strain between the two, as was the case with the majority of the Lookouts and Lucy.

"You had better be very, *very* careful," warned Muriel with simulated cautiousness.

"I intend to be. I may not even speak to you, once I am on the campus," was the retort.

"Oh, it will be safe to speak to me," Muriel assured. "You may even speak to others when you are spoken to and be safe. You are not strictly of the information-bureau type. Don't worry about being afraid of the Hamiltonites. They will probably stand in awe of you."

"What is all this advice you are giving Lucy?" From across the aisle Marjorie leaned toward the quartette in the double seat. "Since it was my turn to be exiled across the aisle, I've lost a lot of pearls of speech."

As only four could occupy the double seat, the five girls had arranged on entraining, to take turns sitting in the seat opposite their own. This was somewhat lonely for the fifth member of the party. The exclusive isolation of the chair car had not found favor with them. They preferred the more democratic day coach where they could be together. While Marjorie could catch little of Muriel's remarks to Lucy, she knew by the half-amused smile on Lucy's face that she was being chaffed and enjoying it.

"Oh, I am simply reassuring Lucy. Now that we are almost in sight of our Mecca, she is beginning to be scared."

"A nice kind of reassurance," scoffed Lucy. "She

just finished telling me the grind hunters would lie in wait for me and to look out for them."

"We'll protect you, Lucy," promised Marjorie lightly. "When we leave the train we will walk two on each side of you. Then you will be safe from——"

"Stretch-your-necks, wags and grind hunters," supplied Jerry, now sufficiently aroused to join in the conversation.

"Something like that. So glad to have you with us again, Jeremiah. We must have bored you terribly or you wouldn't have gone to sleep." Marjorie had adopted Muriel's methods.

"Oh, I can't say I was bored more than usual," drawled Jerry, with a languid wave of her hand. "You are all about the same as ever. No relief in sight before next June. I must do the best I can. In the words of good old Proffy Fontaine: 'No wan can do mo-rr-rr!'" Jerry's imitation of the sorely-tried French professor evoked a chorus of reminiscent giggles.

"Much obliged for your high opinion of our society," said Veronica. "All we can do is to trail around after you, hopeful that someday you will discover how brilliant we really are."

"You may hope," graciously permitted Jerry. "If I discover signs of brilliancy sprouting in any of you, I'll let you know instantly. I won't keep the precious knowledge to myself. There's nothing stingy about me."

"Thank you, thank you," was the united, grateful answer, ending in a burst of low-toned laughter which caused several older persons to smile indulgently upon the bevy of merry-faced girls.

Nine o'clock that morning had seen the five travelers to Hamilton playing their parts at the Sanford station, surrounded by their families and a number of devoted friends. It was not a large crowd that had gathered at the nine-twenty train, but it was a loyal one.

Marjorie had felt very sad and solemn during that last brief wait for the train which was to bear her from home and her own. When it had arrived she had made brave farewells to her captain and general. She had fought hard to keep a smile on her face. Complete control of her emotions returned from a sudden mishap to Jerry. An unexpected jarring of the train threw Jerry off her balance as she was about to deposit a traveling bag in the rack above her head. With a forward lurch, she described a wavering semi-circle in the air with the bag. Banging it down on Muriel's lap, she sprawled helplessly between Muriel and Veronica.

Her timely spill turned the tide of mourning into mirth. Marjorie forgot her sadness, for the time being, in listening with laughter to Jerry's scathing remarks on the subject of trains.

Now, after the greater part of the day spent on the cars, the somewhat tired Lookouts were nearing their journey's end. Fifteen minutes and the town of Hamilton would be reached. Marjorie was wondering, as she idly glimpsed the passing scenery from the car window, if there were many other Hamilton-bound girls on the train. There were only one or two young girls besides her party in the car they were occupying.

"West Hamilton, children," announced Muriel oracularly. "Observe, if you please, the charming beauty of this little burg." She took on the tone of a hired guide. "One of the most picturesque spots in the United States. We will pretend it is, anyway."

"Nothing like having a vivid imagination," murmured Ronny.

"Quite true Miss Lynne," beamed Muriel. "So glad you appreciate my abilities. You are so different in that respect from some girls." She fixed a significant eye upon Jerry, who merely grinned lazily. "Before I go further in expiating on the scenery of this place, one quarter, please, all around. You pay me another quarter after you've seen the town. Just recall that it takes breath and patience to be a successful guide."

"Yes, I guess so," scoffed Jerry. "Kindly tell me where you get the word *guide* as applying to you. A guide is one who guides. All your guiding is done in your mind. I wouldn't pay ten cents to see this town at present. I can see it later for nothing. On to Hamilton! That's my watchword."

"I couldn't see much of it, guide or no guide," remarked Lucy. "The train went so fast, I'm amazed that Muriel could see it well enough to describe the scenery."

"That's something we will let Guide Muriel explain before she collects any of our precious quarters," decreed Jerry.

"I'll do no explaining, and don't you call me Guide Muriel. Start that and it will stick to me. I can't shake it off as I did that old rosette. I see that you and Ronny are determined to make trouble for me. I think I had better keep very quiet from now on."

"Just think what a restful time we might all have had if you had only decided to do that an hour or two earlier," declared Jerry regretfully. "As it is, we are *so* tired. I suppose you must be tired, too?" She beamed questioningly on Muriel, who beamed on her in satirical return, wholly unabashed.

"We are five weary travelers," said Veronica, "about to be dumped down in the strange country of college."

"I like that idea," approved Lucy Warner, with the sudden crispness which marked her speech. "I like to fancy us as five travelers in the country of college. We might call ourselves that." Her eyes darkened with the interest of her own suggestion. "I mean, just in private. There is a certain touch of romance about it that pleases me."

"I like it, too, Lucy," commended Muriel. "I know something we could do as the five travelers, too. Once a week we could meet in one another's rooms, in the evening, and we could each tell how everything has been for us during the week. Whatever happens, we could agree to keep strictly to ourselves until then. That is, unless it were something that had to be settled at once. In that way we would be certain to keep clear of any silly misunderstandings among ourselves. Close friends that we are, none of us is infallible, you know. We know we are not going to quarrel, of course, but a misunderstanding is different. It crops up when you least expect it."

"I'm filled with admiration for you, clever Muriel," praised Veronica. "I wish you hadn't ruined that pretty rosette I made you. I would decorate you all over again. Shall we become the United Order of the Five Travelers? We shall. Our rooms will serve as a wayside inn where we shall gather to tell our tales of joy, woe or adventure.

Do tell Marjorie about it. There she sits by her
sweet little self, with no idea of the great work
going on under her very nose. Here, I'll tell her
myself."

Slipping past Muriel, Ronny crossed the aisle and
touched Marjorie on the shoulder. Unable to hear
with comfort what was being said by her chums,
Marjorie had briefly leaned back in her chair and
closed her eyes. The excitement of the day was
beginning to tell on her. She was feeling dispir-
ited. What a long time it had been since she had
said good-bye to Captain and General! And yet it
was now only late afternoon of the same day.

"Move over," genially ordered Ronny. "I've
something to report, Lieutenant, and only about five
minutes to report it in. We are in sight of the fateful town of Hamilton."

Marjorie obeyed the order, brightening visibly at
Ronny's invasion. "I saw you four with your
heads together," she returned. "I knew something
was stirring."

"I beg to inform you that you are now a member
of the United Order of the Five Travelers," Ronny
announced, dropping her arm over Marjorie's
shoulder. Rapidly she repeated what had been
talked over across the aisle. Marjorie listened in
absorption. Her quick brain instantly grasped the
value of the project from its ethical side. It would

be good for all of them, she thought, to have these little confidence sessions. It would be the very best thing in the world for Lucy.

"Hamilton! Hamil-lton-n-n!" The stentorian call echoed through the car. Their interest centered on the new idea, both girls were startled by the brakeman's loud tones.

"I must gather up my luggage." Ronny sprang up and hurriedly sought her own seat with: "More later about the Five Travelers."

Marjorie nodded and began mechanically to gather up her own luggage. It consisted of a suit case and a smart leather hand bag across the aisle. The box of candied fruit, presented to her by Mr. La Salle, was going the rounds for the last time. It had been mischievously started by Muriel and smilingly declined by three canny freshmen.

"You don't catch me marching out of the train with my mouth full of candy, looking as though I were about seven years old," was Jerry's decided stand. "Go ahead. Eat some yourself, Muriel."

"I don't think it would be polite to eat all of Marjorie's candy," declined Muriel.

"The delicate consideration of that girl! Ahem! Here's your candy, Sweet Marjoram." Reaching over, Jerry deposited it on Marjorie's seat. "Now for a first timid look at Collegeburg!" As the train began to slow down for a dead stop, Jerry peered curiously out of the car window.

From her own window, Marjorie was also casting her first glances at the Hamilton station. Like the stations of exclusive suburban towns, adjacent to large cities, this one had two separate station buildings; one for outgoing and the other for incoming trains. The two connected by a stone passage-way underneath, ascent or descent made possible by a short flight of stone steps at each end of the passage.

As it happened, Marjorie had been sitting on the side of the car that faced toward the outgoing trains. In consequence, her first impression of Hamilton was a blank. She had expected to see groups of girls in white and light-colored gowns walking up and down the platform. She had looked forward to a scene of moving color and young life. Now all she saw was a platform, empty save for an elderly man, who was leading a little boy of perhaps five or six years along it. This surely was not the Hamilton of her dreams.

CHAPTER IX.

A DISAPPOINTMENT AND A FRIEND.

A MOMENT later she was moving out of the train
with her chums, smiling over her recent flat sense
of disappointment. A glance out of a window on
the opposite side of the car had proved reassuring.
On the platform toward which she and her friends
were directing their steps were girls in abundance.

"Look at the mob!" Jerry made this low-tone
exclamation over her shoulder as she went down
the car steps.

Soon the Five Travelers had left the car behind
them and become a part of the throng on the station
platform. Unconsciously they drew together in a
compact, little bunch, somewhat as a quintette of
homeless kittens might have done, who had been
thrown out on a very big, inhospitable world to
wonder what was going to happen to them next.

There they continued to stand for at least three
minutes, each busily forming her own opinions of
this particular feature of college life. Two girls who
had left the train just ahead of them had already

been pounced upon by a group of their friends and whisked off the platform. At the right of them a tall, dignified girl in glasses was shaking hands warmly with three welcoming friends. She looked as though she might be a senior. It was not until long afterward that Marjorie learned that she was a prospective freshman who failed ignominiously in her entrance examinations and left Hamilton, disconsolate.

The longer they stood and watched what went on around them, the more it became enforced upon them that there was a welcome for everyone but themselves.

"I am afraid they didn't get our telegram," commented Jerry, with a degree of sarcasm that bespoke her contempt for everything she had ever heard or read of college hospitality and tradition.

"Our telegram? Why, did you send a——? Oh, I see." Muriel Harding shrewdly surveyed the scene before her, a glint of belligerence in her eyes.

"Of course I didn't send a telegram. Can't you tell when I am sarcastic? I supposed I was extremely sarcastic just then. I'll have to try again." The fact of being ignored by the upper class students of Hamilton had not disturbed Jerry's ever ready sense of humor.

"Come on, girls." Ronny spoke almost authoritatively. "We know our destination is Wayland

Hall and it is on the campus. We can find a taxi-cab easily enough. We don't have to wait for a reception committee, apparently not on duty today."

"Shades of the Students' Aid where art thou?" declaimed Marjorie, the tiniest touch of satire in the remark.

"Humph! I must say that I am not so particular about that minus welcome. Fortunately we are neither children nor idiots. I think we can find our way without any help."

With this sturdy assertion Jerry lifted her suit-case from the platform and gazed defiantly about her. The others followed her example, and the five girls headed for a short set of stone steps at the back of the platform which formed an exit from the station premises. In order to reach the steps they had to wind their way in and out of the groups of young women which filled the platform. Several pairs of bright eyes were turned on them for the conventional, well-bred second, yet none came forward to speak to them.

As Veronica had predicted, it was no trouble to find a taxicab. Two or three dark blue cabs, be-longing to the railroad company, were drawn up in the open space behind the station. Selecting the first one they came to, Veronica gave the driver the address, and the Five Travelers stepped into the automobile.

As they drove out of the station yard they passed a large gray car driving in. It was filled to overflowing with girls, all of them in high spirits. Marjorie noted as the car glided by her that the girl at the wheel was particularly attractive. Even a passing glance revealed that fact. A little ache tugged at her heart. It seemed rather hard that they should have been so utterly ignored.

"Now that I've seen some of these dear little children of our Alma Mater, I'm better pleased with myself than ever. Let me tell you one thing and that isn't two," Jerry paused impressively, "they need reforming badly. But don't you ask me to tackle the job. I feel in my aristocratic bones that I owe it to myself to be very exclusive this year; and *I am going to be it.*"

"I don't care to know anyone except you girls." Lucy Warner looked almost pleased at the prospect of forming no new acquaintances at college.

"I don't like the idea of being slighted," Muriel complained. "I can't say that I expected to have a fuss made over me. Still, we Lookouts have been at the head of things so much in Sanford High that it hurts to be passed by entirely. Besides, I wish to like college. I would not be content to go on all year without meeting *some* pleasant girls with whom I could be friendly. You know what I mean."

Muriel looked almost appealingly about her. The five girls had tucked themselves into the tonneau of the machine, three on the main seat and two occupying the small chair-like stools opposite. Her eyes rested last on Marjorie whose meditative expression promised support.

Thus far, none of the travelers had paid the slightest attention to the clean, well laid out town of Hamilton through which they were passing. They were too wholly concerned at the utter lack of courtesy which had been accorded them. It brushed Veronica least of all. Her experience of the previous year had made her case-hardened. While Lucy was not anxious to make new acquaintances, she did not like to see the others ignored. Jerry, Muriel and Marjorie had, however, been cut to the quick.

"I feel queer over it," was Marjorie's candid admission. "It is just as though some one had given poor old Hamilton College a hard slap. It is not according to the tradition of any really fine college to forego hospitality. Why, you will recall, Ronny, Miss Archer was telling us that one of the oldest traditions of Hamilton was 'Remember the stranger within thy gates.' I thought that so beautiful. Different girls I know, who have gone to college, have told me that there was always a committee of students to meet the principal trains and make things comfortable for entering freshmen.

"We didn't go about matters scientifically," Jerry asserted. "We should have seen to it that the railroad company posted a large bulletin in front of the station announcing us something like this: 'Sanford High School takes pleasure in announcing the arrival at Hamilton, on the five-fifty train, of the following galaxy of shining stars: Veronica Browning Lynne, Millionairess; Lucy Eleanor Warner, Valedictorian, i. e., extra brilliant; Muriel Harding, Howling Beauty and Basketball Artist; Marjorie Dean, Marvelous Manager of Everyone; Jeremiah Macy, Politician and Fat Girl. A full turn out of all college societies and classes is requested in order to fitly welcome this noted quintette. Orchestra take notice. Brass Band must be present in dress uniform.' "

Jerry drew a long breath as she concluded, then giggled softly as the absurdity of her own conception struck her.

"Honestly, Jerry Macy, you are the limit. Do you or do you not care that nobody has cared enough for us to show us the ordinary college courtesies?" Muriel's question was half laughing, half vexed.

"Oh, I am not made of wood," Jerry retorted. "Still I am not so grieved that I won't be able to eat my dinner, provided the doors of Wayland Hall aren't slammed in our faces. By the way, what does this town look like? I have been so busy with our united sorrows that I forgot to inspect it."

Jerry turned her attention to the broad, smooth street through which the taxicab was passing. They were traveling through the prettiest part of Hamilton, the handsome stone residences on each side of the street with the close-cropped stretches of lawn, denoting the presence of luxury. Against the vivid green of the grass, scarlet sage flaunted its gorgeous color in carefully laid out bed or border. Cannas, dahlias and caladiums lent tropical effect to middle-state topography. Here and there the early varieties of garden chrysanthemums were in bloom, their pink, white and bronze beauty adding to the glorious color schemes which autumn knows best how to paint. Nor did the little piles of fallen leaves that dotted the lawns, brown heaps against the green, detract from the picture.

Continuing for some distance along the street which was now claiming their attention, the car turned into another street, equally ornamental. Soon they noticed that the houses were growing farther apart and more after the fashion of country estates. There were immense sweeps of velvety lawn, shaded by trees large and small of numerous variety. The residences, too, were veritable castles. Situated far back from the thoroughfare, they were often just visible through their protecting leafy screen.

"We can't be far from Hamilton." It was Veronica who broke the brief silence that had fallen on them as their appreciative eyes took in the beauty spread lavishly along their route. "The Hamilton bulletin says the college is a little over two miles from the station. These beautiful country houses, that we have been passing, belong to what is called the Hamilton Estates, I imagine. The bulletin speaks of the Hamilton Estates in describing the college, you know."

"Yes; it said that Brooke Hamilton, the founder of Hamilton College, once owned all the country around here. One of these estates is called Hamilton Arms," supplemented Marjorie. "It said so little about this Brooke Hamilton. I would have liked to know more of his history. He must have been a true gentleman of the old school. It mentions that many of the finest traditions of Hamilton College were oft repeated sayings of his. So he must have been a noble man."

"Well, I am only sorry that he wasn't on hand to welcome us," regretted Jerry, the irrepressible. "Now you needn't be shocked at my levity. I meant seriously that he was really needed today."

"Look!" The single word of exclamation from Lucy centered all eyes to where she was pointing.

Upon their view had burst the wide, gently undulating green slopes of Hamilton Campus. While the grounds surrounding the majority of institutions of learning are laid out with an eye to the decorative, Hamilton campus has a peculiar, living charm of its own that perhaps none other has ever possessed. It is not that its thick short grass grows any greener than that of other campuses. Still it is more pleasing to the eye. The noble growth of elm, beech and maple, shading the lawns at graceful distances apart carries a personality that one feels but can hardly express by description.

Ornamental shrubs there are in tasteful plenty, but not in profusion. It is as though nothing grows on that immense, rolling tract of land that is not necessary to the picture formed by natural beauty and intensified by intelligent landscape-gardening. Even the stately gray stone buildings, which stand out at intervals on the broad field of green, bear the same stamp of individuality.

"It is wonderful!" Lucy spoke in an awed voice. The majesty of the scene had gripped her hard.

"How beautiful!" The spell was on Ronny, too. She was gazing across the emerald stretches with half-closed, worshipping eyes. "My own dear West is wonderful, but there is something about this that touches one's heart. I never feel quite that way when I look out at the mountains or the California valleys, dear as they are to me."

"I love it all!" Marjorie's wide brown eyes had grown larger with emotion. She was meeting for the first time one that would later be her steadfast friend, changing only from one beauty to another —Hamilton Campus.

* * *

CHAPTER X.

AN AMIABLE SOPHOMORE.

"I cannot really help but feel that there must have been a mistake about our being ignored at the station." Marjorie made this hopeful remark just as the taxicab passed through a wide driveway and swung into a drive that wound a circuitous course about the campus. "It is hard to believe that any student of this beloved old college wouldn't be ready and willing to look after freshman strays like us."

"I am afraid times have changed since Mr. Brooke Hamilton laid down the laws of courtesy," Veronica made sceptical reply. "Beg your pardon, Sweet Marjoram, I should not have said that. I am just as much in love with Hamilton Campus as you are. I regret to say, I haven't the same generous faith in Hamilton's upper classmen. There has been a shirking of duty somewhere among them. I know a receiving committee when I see one, and there was none on that station platform, for I took a good look over it. I saw a number of students greeting others that they had come to the station purposely to meet, but that is all. Sounds disagreeably positive, doesn't it? I do not mean to be so, though."

"I can't blame you for the way you feel about the whole business, Ronny," Marjorie returned. We had all looked forward to the pleasure of being taken under the wing of a friendly upper class girl until we knew our way about a little. Well, it didn't happen, so there is no use in my mourning or spurting or worrying about it. I am going to forget it."

" ' 'Twere wiser to forget,' quoted Ronny. Her brief irritation vanishing, her face broke into smiling beauty. " 'Don't give up the ship.' That's another quotation, appropriate to you, Marjorie. You aren't going to let such grouches as Jeremiah and I spoil your belief in the absent sophs and juniors. The seniors usually leave the welcoming job to them. Of course, there are a few seniors who have the freshmen's welfare upon their consciences."

The taxicab was now slowing down for a stop

before a handsome four-story house of gray stone. It stood on what might be termed the crest of the campus, almost on a level with a very large building, a hundred rods away, which the newcomers guessed to be Hamilton Hall. An especially roomy and ornamental veranda extended around three sides of the first story of the house. Its tasteful wicker and willow chairs and tables, and large, comfortable-looking porch swings made it appear decidedly attractive to the somewhat disillusioned arriving party. Their new home, at least, was not a disappointment.

The lawns about the house were no less beautiful with autumn glory than those they had already seen. Marjorie in particular was charmed by the profusion of chrysanthemums, the small, old-fashioned variety of garden blooms. There were thick, blossoming clumps of them at the rounding corners of the veranda. They stood in the sturdy, colorful array as borders to two wide walks that led away from entrances to the Hall on both sides. At the left of the Hall, toward the rear of it, was an oblong bed of them, looking old-fashioned enough in its compact formation to have been planted by Brooke Hamilton himself.

The drive led straight up to the house, stopping in an open space in front of the veranda, wide enough to permit an automobile to turn comfortably. It was here that the Five Travelers alighted, bag and baggage.

"I wonder if we are early at college. The place seems to be deserted. Maybe our fellow residents are at dinner. No, they are not. It is only twenty minutes past six." Jerry consulted her wrist watch. "The Hamilton bulletin states the dinner hour at Wayland Hall to be at six-thirty until the first of November. After that six o'clock until the first of April; then back to six-thirty again."

"It would not surprise me to hear that a good share of the students who live at Wayland Hall had not yet returned. According to our valued bulletin,—we have to fall back on it for information,— Wayland Hall is the oldest campus house. That would make it desirable in the eyes of upper class girls. We were fortunate to obtain reservations here."

They had crossed the open space in front of the house and mounted the steps. As they reached the doorway a girl stepped out of it. So sudden was her appearance that she narrowly missed colliding with the arrivals. She had evidently hurried out of a reception room at the left of the hall. Passing through the hall or coming down the open staircase she would have seen the group before reaching the door.

"Oh, I beg your pardon," she apologized, viewing

the newcomers out of a pair of very blue, non-curi-
ous eyes. "I never pay proper attention to where
I am going. I was so busy thinking about an examination I must take tomorrow that I forgot where
I was. I'll have to stop now for a second to remember what I started out to do," she added ruefully,
her face breaking into a roguish smile which displayed two pronounced dimples.

Instantly the hearts of the Five Travelers warmed
toward her. Her dimples brought back fond mem-
ories of Susan Atwell. She was quite a tall girl,
five feet, seven inches, at least, and very slender.
Her hair was a pale flaxen and fluffed out naturally, worn severely back from her low forehead
though it was. Her one-piece frock of white wash
satin gave her a likeness to a tall white June lily,
nodding contentedly on a sturdy stem.

"I wonder if I can be of service to you," she said
quickly. Courtesy had not deserted her. *She* could,
it seemed, pay proper attention to the needs of the
stranger.

"I wish you would be so kind as to tell us where
we will find Miss Remson. We are entering freshmen, and are to live at Wayland Hall." Marjorie
introduced herself and friends to the other girl, stat-
ing also from whence they had come.

"Oh, you are the Sanford crowd!" exclaimed the
girl. "Why, Miss Weyman was to meet you at the

train! She went down to the garage for her car. Two sophomores from her club, the Sans Soucians, were to go down with her to the five-fifty train. They left here in plenty of time for I saw them go. They must have missed making connections with you somehow. I forgot to introduce myself. I am Helen Trent of the sophomore class."

The Lookouts having expressed their pleasure in meeting this amiable member of the sophomore class, Miss Trent led the way inside and ushered them into the reception room. It was a medium-sized room, done in two shades of soft brown and furnished with a severely beautiful set of golden oak, upholstered in brown leather. The library table was littered with current magazines, giving the apartment the appearance of a physician's receiving room.

Seized by a sudden thought, Jerry turned to their new acquaintance and asked: "Does the Miss Weyman you spoke of drive a large gray car?"

"Why, yes." Helen Trent opened her blue eyes a trifle wider in patent surprise. She was speculating as to whether it would be within bounds to inquire how the questioner had come by her knowledge.

Jerry saved her the interrogation. "Then we saw her, just as we drove out of the station yard. She was driving this gray car I mentioned. It looked to me like a French car. There must have been seven or eight girls in it besides herself."

"It was Natalie you saw. There isn't another car like hers here at Hamilton. It is a French car."

Jerry turned to Marjorie, a positive grin over-spreading her plump face. "Right you were, wise Marjorie, about the mistake business. Perhaps time may restore our shattered faith in the Hamiltonites. What did you say Veronica?" She beamed mischievously at Ronny.

"I did not say a single word," retorted Ronny. "I am glad Marjorie was right, though."

Helen Trent stood listening, her eyes betraying frank amusement at Jerry, her dimples threatening to break out again.

"We were a little bit disappointed because not a soul spoke to us after we left the train. We had looked forward to having a few Hamilton upper classmen, if only one or two, speak to us. Perhaps we were silly to expect it. To me it seemed one of the nicest features of going to college. I said I thought there must have been a mistake about no one meeting us. That is what Geraldine meant."

Marjorie made this explanation with the candor of a child. Her brown eyes met Helen's so sweetly and yet so steadfastly, as she talked, that the sophomore thought her the prettiest girl she had ever seen. Helen's sympathies had enlisted toward the entire five. Even Lucy Warner had struck her as a girl of great individuality. A slow smile touched the corners of her lips, seemingly the only outward manifestation of some inner cogitation that was mildly amusing.

"I am glad, too, that it was a mistake," she said, her face dropping again into its soft placidity. "We wish our freshmen friends to think well of us. We sophs are only a year ahead of you. It is particularly our duty to help the freshmen when first they come to Hamilton. I would have gone down to the station today to meet you but Natalie Weyman took it upon herself. I have this special exam. to take. I have been preparing for it this summer. It is in trigonometry. I failed in that subject last term and had to make it up this vacation. I only hope I pass in it tomorrow. Br—r—r! the very idea makes me shiver."

"I hope you will, I am sure." It was Ronny who expressed this sincere wish. She had quickly decided that she approved of Helen Trent. Certainly there was nothing snobbish about her. She showed every mark of gentle breeding.

"I am afraid we may be keeping you from what you were about to do when we stopped you." Lucy Warner had stepped to the fore much to the secret amazement of her friends. A stickler for duty,

Lucy's training as secretary had taught her the value of time. During that period that she spent in Miss Archer's office, her own time had been so seriously encroached upon that she had made a resolution never to waste that of others.

"Oh, no; I can pick up my own affairs again, later. None of them are important except my exam., and I am not going to worry over that. If you will excuse me, I will go and find Miss Remson. She will assign you to your rooms. Dinner is on now. There goes the bell. It is later this one week; at a quarter to seven, on account of returning students. It's on until a quarter to eight. Beginning next week, it will be on at precisely half-past six and off at half-past seven. After that you go hungry, or else to Baretti's or the Colonial. Both are quite near here. No more explanation now, but action."

With a pleasant little nod the sophomore left the reception room in search of Miss Remson, the manager of Wayland Hall. She left behind her, however, an atmosphere of friendliness and cheer that went far toward dispelling the late cloud of having been either purposely or carelessly overlooked.

CHAPTER XI.

SETTLING DOWN AT WAYLAND HALL.

"Yes; to be sure. I have the correspondence from all of you Sanford girls. I think there has been no mistake concerning your rooms. Just a moment."

Miss Remson, a small, wiry-looking woman with a thin, pleasant face and partially gray hair, bustled to a door, situated at the lower end of the room. Thrown open, it disclosed a small, inner apartment, evidently doing duty as the manager's office. Seating herself before a flat-topped oak desk, she opened an upper drawer and took from it a fat, black, cloth-covered book. Consulting it, she rose and returned with it in her hand.

"Miss Dean and Miss Macy made application for one room together, Miss Harding for a single room, provided a classmate, who expected to enter Wellesley, did not change her mind in favor of Hamilton. In that case she would occupy the room with Miss Harding. Miss Lynne applied for a single and afterward made request that Miss Warner might share it with her. Am I correct?"

The manager spoke in an alert tone, looking up
with a slight sidewise slant of her head that reminded
Marjorie of a bird.

"That is the way we meant it to be. I hope
there have been no changes in the programme."
Jerry had constituted herself spokesman.

"None, whatever. I have a request to make of
Miss Harding." Unerringly she picked out Muriel,
though Marjorie had only gone over their names to
her once by way of general introduction. "Would
you be willing to take a room-mate? We have so
many applications for Wayland Hall to which we
simply can pay no attention save to return the word
'no room.' This particular application of which I
speak has been made by a junior, Miss Hortense
Barlow. She was at Wayland Hall during her
freshman year, but left here to room with a friend
at Acasia House during her sophomore year. Her
friend was a junior then and was therefore graduated last June. Miss Barlow is most anxious to
return to this house."

Muriel looked rather blank at this disclosure.
She was not at all anxious for a room-mate, unless
it were a Lookout, which was out of the question.

"I hardly know yet whether I should care to take
a room-mate," she said, with a touch of hesitation.
"I will decide tonight and let you know tomorrow
morning. Will that be satisfactory?"

"Perfectly, perfectly," responded Miss Remson, and waved her hand as though urbanely to dismiss the subject. "I will show you young women to your rooms myself. Dinner, this week, is from a quarter to seven until a quarter to eight." She repeated the information already given them by Helen Trent. "That means that no one will be admitted to the dining room after a quarter to eight. We are making special allowances now on account of returning students."

With this she led the way out of the reception room and up the stairs. Down the hall of the second story she went, with a brisk little swishing of her black taffeta skirt that reminded Marjorie more then ever of a bird. At the last door on the left of the hall she paused.

"This is the room Miss Lynne and Miss Warner are to occupy," she announced. "Directly across find the room Miss Macy and Miss Dean are to occupy. She turned abruptly and indicated the door opposite. Miss Harding's room is on the third floor. I will conduct you to it, Miss Harding. I trust you will like your new quarters, young ladies, and be happy in them."

Immediately she turned with "Follow me, Miss Harding," and was off down the hall. It was a case of go without delay or lose her guide. Making a funny little grimace behind the too-brisk manager's back, Muriel called, "See you later," and set off in haste after Miss Remson. She had already reached the foot of the staircase leading to the third story.

"She's the busiest busybody ever, isn't she?" remarked Jerry. Marjorie, Ronny and Lucy at her back, she opened the door of her room and stepped over the threshold. "Hmm!" she next held forth. "This place may not be the lap of luxury, but it is not so bad. I don't see my pet Circassian walnut set or my dear comfy old window seat, with about a thousand, more or less, nice downy pillows. Still it's no barn. I only hope those couch beds are what they ought to be, a place on which to sleep. They're more ornamental to a room than the regulation bed. I suppose that's why they're here."

"Stop making fun of things, you goose, and let's get the dust washed off our hands and faces before we go down to dinner. I am smudgy, and also very hungry, and it is almost seven o'clock," Marjorie warned. "We haven't a miute to lose. A person as methodical as Miss Remson would close the dining room door in our faces if we were a fraction of a minute late."

"Don't doubt it. Good-bye." Veronica made a dive for her quarters followed by Lucy.

"You and I *will* certainly have to hurry," agreed Jerry, as she returned from the lavatory nearly twenty minutes later. Marjorie, who had preceded her, was just finishing the redressing of her hair. It rippled away from her forehead and broke into shining little curls about her ears and at the nape of her neck. Her eyes bright with the excitement of new surroundings and her cheeks aglow from her recent ablutions, her loveliness was startling.

"I won't have time to do my hair over again," Jerry lamented. "It will have to go as it is. Are you ready? Come on, then. We'll stop for Ronny and Lucy. What of Muriel? Last seen she was piking off after Miss Busy Buzzy. Hasn't *she* the energy though? B-z-z-z-z! Away she goes. I hope she never hears me call her that. I might go to the foot of the stairway and howl 'Muriel' but that would hardly be well-bred."

"She will probably stop for us. You can't lose Muriel." Marjorie was still smiling over Jerry's disrespectful name for the manager. "For goodness' sake, Jerry, be careful about calling her that. Don't let it go further than among the Five Travelers. We understand that it is just your funny self. If some outsider heard it and you tried to explain yourself—well, you couldn't."

"I know that all too well, dear old Mentor. I'll be careful. Don't worry about me, as little Charlie Stevens says after he has run away and Gray Gables has been turned upside down hunting him.

I presume that is Muriel now." A decided rapping
sent Jerry hurrying to the door. About to make
some humorous remark to Muriel concerning her
late hasty disappearance, she caught herself in time.
Three girls were grouped outside the door but they
were not the expected trio of Lookouts.

CHAPTER XII.

UNEXPECTED CALLERS.

"Good evening," Jerry managed to say politely,
amazed though she was at the unlooked-for callers.

"Good evening," came the prompt response from
the foremost girl, spoken in a cool velvety tone that
somehow suggested patronage. "Are you Miss
Dean?"

"No, I am Miss Macy. Miss Dean is my room-
mate. She is here. Will you come in?"

"Thank you." The caller stepped into the room,
her two companions at her heels. She was a young
woman of about the same height as Marjorie and
not unlike her in coloring, save that her eyes were a
bluish gray, shaded by long dark lashes, her eye-
brows heavily marked. Her hair, a paler brown
than Marjorie's, suggested in arrangement a hair-

dresser's art rather than that of natural beauty, pleasing though the coiffure was. Her frock of pale pink and white effects in silk net and taffeta was cut short enough of sleeve and low enough of neck to permit the white shapeliness of her arms and shoulders to be seen. While her features might be called regular, a close observer would have pronounced her mouth, in repose, a shade too small for the size of her face, and her chin a trifle too pointed.

Standing as she was where the electric lights, which Jerry had recently switched on, played upon her, she made an undeniably attractive picture. Marjorie recognized her instantly as the girl she had seen driving the gray car. One of her companions was a small, dark girl with very black eyes and a sulky mouth. She was wearing a gown of Nile green pongee, heavily trimmed with expensive ecru lace. It gave her the appearance of being actually weighed down. The third of the callers Marjorie took an instant dislike toward. She represented a type of girl that Marjorie had rarely seen and never encountered at Sanford High School.

While her companions were attired in evening frocks, she was wearing a sports suit of a white woolly material that was a marvel as to cut and finish. The white silk velour sports hat, the heavy white silk stockings and fine, stitched buckskin ties that completed her costume were the acme of dis-

tinctive expense. Despite her carefully chosen apparel, she was very near to possessing an ugliness
of face and feature which no amount of smart
clothes could mitigate. Her hair, such as could be
seen of it from under her hat, was coarse and black.
Small, shrewd brown eyes, which had a trick of
half closing, high cheek bones, a rather retroussé
nose and a large, loose-lipped mouth completed an
outer personality that Marjorie found unprepossess-
ing in the extreme. Last of the three to enter the
room, she had closed the door and now stood
almost lounging against it, eyeing Marjorie with a
smile that suggested bored tolerance.

"I am Marjorie Dean." Immediately she heard
her name, Marjorie had come forward. She guessed
that the girl of the gray car had come to offer an
apology for her non-appearance. Memory furnish-
ing her with the spokesman's name, she held out her
hand courteously, saying: "Your are Miss Weyman,
are you not? Won't you and your friends sit
down?"

Into Natalie Weyman's darkening eyes flared an
expression of affronted surprise. The little dark
girl also showed surprise, while the girl in the
sports suit drew down the corners of her wide
mouth as though she had heard something funny
but dared not laugh outright.

"Yes, I am Natalie Weyman." Whatever her

thoughts were her tones were still velvety. "I am a sophomore and these are my sophy pals, Miss Vale and Miss Cairns. She indicated first the small girl, then the lounger. Both sophomores bowed nonchalantly and lightly clasped the hand Marjorie extended to each in turn.

"This is my room-mate and very dear friend, Geraldine Macy." Marjorie now took her turn at introducing.

Jerry bowed and shook hands with the trio, but exhibited no enthusiasm. She was inwardly raging at them for having chosen a time so inopportune for making a call. She felt like shouting out in a loud, terrifying voice: "Have you had your dinner? Well, we haven't had ours. Now beat it, all of you!"

Introductions over, the callers sat down. Miss Weyman dropped gracefully into the nearest easy chair, of which the room could count two. The others seated themselves, side by side, on one of the couch beds. Hardly had they done so when a second rapping was heard. This time it was Veronica, Lucy and Muriel. Marjorie opened the door and said quickly: "Come in, girls. I wish you to meet three members of the sophomore class who have done us the honor to call."

Involuntarily Veronica's eloquent eyebrows went up in surprise. Lucy's green eyes took on a peculiar gleam, and Muriel felt displeasure rising within her. It seemed too bad that, after being neglected, they should be thus sought before they had had time to get their dinner. The long ride on the train had left them hungry. Still, there was nothing to be done save make the best of it. How long the callers had been in Marjorie's and Jerry's room, Muriel could not know. If they took prompt leave the Sanford five could still get into the dining room before it closed. It was twenty minutes to eight. She had looked at her watch while Ronny was rapping on the door.

After further introductions Miss Weyman said sweetly: "I have an apology to make Miss Dean. Consider it as being made to all of you. I was to meet you at the train today, and unfortunately I started a little later than I had intended. I belong to a club which a few of the freshmen started last year. All the girls who are members were friends of mine before I entered Hamilton. We attended a *very* private preparatory school and entered college together. We call ourselves the San Soucians and our club is limited to eighteen members. We do not intend to pass it on after we are graduated from Hamilton. It is really only a little social club of our own. Of course, we *try* to be considerate toward the other students here, as in the case of welcoming the freshmen."

"Every one was so perfectly sweet to us last year when we entered Hamilton." Miss Vale now raised a voice in the conversation. "You see we came from New York to Hamilton in my father's private car. My father is president of the L. T. and M. Railroad. We had not thought much about being met at the train by the upper classmen. I *wish* you might have *seen* the crowd that was there to meet us! Girls from *all three classes* turned out. We had a smart old celebration, I can tell you." Her sulky mouth lost its droop as she went on to describe boastingly the glories of that particular reception. She ended with: "What prep. school do you come from?"

Informed by Jerry that the Five Travelers were graduated from high school, she glanced pityingly about the Sanford group, and subsided with: "I really know nothing at all about high schools. I did not suppose you could enter college from one."

"Of course one can." Veronica spoke with an energy that her friends understood, if the callers did not. "Let me ask you a question. Were you obliged to try entrance examinations to Hamilton College?"

"Ye—s." The reply came a little slowly.

"We are not obliged to take examinations. The senior course in our high school comprises collegiate subjects. Our diplomas will admit us to any college in the United States. So you see that high school has at least that advantage," Ronny concluded evenly.

"I have heard that some of those high schools are really excellent," drawled Miss Cairns. "I have heard too that they turn out a lot of digs and prigs. Girls, you understand, that have to get all they can out of high school because college is out of the question for them. I feel sorry for them. I never knew any of that sort, though. In fact, you are the first high school girls I have ever met. What?" She turned to Natalie Weyman.

The latter, however, was paying little attention to the conversation. Her gaze had rested almost uninterruptedly on Marjorie since she had entered the room. From the discomfited lieutenant's lovely face to her slender, graceful figure, clothed in a one-piece frock of dark blue crêpe de chine, the other girl's eyes wandered, only to turn themselves away for a moment, then begin a fresh inspection.

Meanwhile time was flying, the Five Travelers were growing minutely hungrier, yet the visitors made no move to go. Miss Weyman had gone no further than to explain that she had started for the train a little late. This apology did not coincide with what Helen Trent had said. None of the Lookouts had forgotten *her* remarks on the subject. It was in each girl's mind that she preferred to believe Helen. This did not argue well as to a future friendship with Natalie Weyman. None of them could endure even the shadow of untruth.

"Please pardon me for breaking into my apology with an explanation of our club." Her inspection of Marjorie over for the present, Natalie returned to the original object of her call. "I meant to say that by the time I had reached the station you had gone on to Wayland Hall, I suppose."

"We drove away from the station in a taxicab just as your car drove into the yard." Muriel fixed the lamely apologetic sophomore with a steady gaze. Her brown eyes appeared to be taking the other's measure.

"Did you, indeed," Natalie returned somewhat hastily. It was beginning to dawn upon her that she did not in the least like any of these freshmen. They were entirely too independent to suit her. Recalling that which she had been aching to ask when Marjorie had asked her if she were Miss Weyman, she now questioned almost rudely: "How did you know who *I* was when you saw me at the station?"

"We did not know who you were then," explained Muriel. "We merely saw a gray car full of girls. Miss Macy said it looked like a French car. Afterward, we met a delightful sophomore, Miss Trent.

In talking with her, she mentioned that you had gone to the station to meet us."

"Oh, yes. Miss Trent. She was on the veranda when we left here." She looked toward Miss Cairns for corroboration. The latter nodded slightly and made an almost imperceptible gesture with her left hand.

"We are so sorry we missed you, at any rate." Miss Vail took it upon herself to do a share of the apologizing. At the same time she rose from her seat on the couch bed. "How do you like the table here?" she queried condescendingly. "We find it better than last year. Remson has a new cook now. She can see the other cook silly when it comes to eats."

A peculiar silence ensued as Miss Vale's high-pitched tones ceased. It had been forced upon the Lookouts to defer an opinion of said "table" until the next day. They were certainly at present in no position to make a statement.

"As we have been here so short a time we can't pass an opinion on a thing at Wayland Hall yet." Marjorie answered for her friends, not daring to look toward any of them.

"Naturally not," agreed Miss Cairns suavely. "Mind if we leave you now? We really must go, Nat. We had our dinner at Baretti's tonight.

Some of the Sans are waiting at the Colonial for us. We are going on there for dessert."

"Yes, the gang will wonder what has become of us." Natalie now got to her feet. She favored the Lookouts with a smile, which was intended to be gracious, but utterly lacked sincerity. Her pals already at the door, she joined them. This time there was no handshaking. While it would not have been necessary, a truly sincere bevy of girls would have undoubtedly shaken hands and enjoyed that act of fellowship.

"Thank you for remembering us at the station today, even though we did miss connections. We appreciate your coming to call on us this evening, too. Freshmen are very lowly persons at college until they have won their spurs on the field of college honors. We shall try not to be an annoyance to our sophomore sisters."

Marjorie tried conscientiously to put aside all trace of irritation as she made this little speech. She realized that her chums had left it to her to handle the situation. While they had all exchanged a certain amount of conversation with the visitors, they had run out from sheer lack of sympathy. The callers had aroused belligerence in Jerry, Ronny and Muriel. Lucy Warner had fairly congealed with dislike. Marjorie had alone stayed on an even keel.

Perhaps the unfailing courtesy of the tired, hungry lieutenant made some slight impression on the departing sophomores. Halfway out the door as Marjorie answered, Natalie Weyman had the grace to say: "You really haven't anything to thank us for, Miss Dean. Wait until we do something for you, worth while. We will drop in on you again when we have more time. Good night."

She had been on the point of offering her hand at the last, stirred out of her usual self-centeredness by Marjorie's gentle manners. Then she had looked again at the freshman's exquisite face, and fellowship had died before birth. Natalie Weyman was considered a beauty at home, in New York City, and at Hamilton College. She had at last seen a girl whom she considered fully as pretty as herself. As a result she was now very, very jealous.

CHAPTER XIII.

ON THE TRAIL OF DINNER.

"CAN you beat it? Uh-h-h-h!" Jerry dropped with angry force into the arm chair which Natalie Weyman had so recently vacated. "What was the matter with those girls, anyway? How could they help but know that we hadn't had our din-

ner? It was after six o'clock when we reached
here. It took time to get hold of Busy Buzzy and
be assigned to our rooms, and more time to make
ourselves presentable. Why couldn't they have figured out that much? Next step in our process of
deduction; they came to the door about twenty
minutes past seven. Now how could we have had
time to go down stairs, eat our dinner and be back
in our room again?"

"The answer is, they didn't do any deducing,"
declared Muriel. "I suppose they simply chose their
own time to call."

"A very inconvenient time, I must say," grumbled Jerry. "Here's another point that needs clearing up. If that Miss Weyman drove her car down
to the station, expecting to bring the five of us back
in it, why was it cram-jam full of girls?"

"They may have been friends of hers who merely
wanted to ride down to the station, Jerry," surmised Ronny. "Why trouble your brain about our
callers now? Let us think about where we are
going to have our dinner. The dining room is
closed, of course. We shall have to call on the hospitable Baretti for sustenance. He's hospitable if
his restaurant is still open. Otherwise, I don't
think much of him."

"First thing to do is to find out where he holds
forth. I hope the place is not far from here. I'm

so hungry and so tired." Marjorie spoke with a tired kind of patience that ended in a yawn. "We had better start out at once. We'll probably find some one downstairs who can direct us."

The others no less hungry, the Five Travelers lost no more time in getting downstairs, preferring to leave the subject of their recent callers until a time more convenient for discussion. At the foot of the stairs they encountered two girls about to ascend.

"Good evening. Will you please direct us to Baretti's?" It was Ronny who asked the question in a clear, even tone that, while courteous, was so strictly impersonal as to be almost cool. Having just encountered a trio of girls whom she had instantly set down as snobs, Ronny had donned her armor.

"Good evening." Both girls returned the salutation. The taller of the two, a sandy-haired young woman with sleepy gray eyes, a square chin and freckles now became spokesman. "You will find Baretti's about a square from the west wall of the campus. Turn to your right as you pass out the main gate."

"There is the Colonial, too, about two squares beyond Baretti's," informed the other, a pretty girl in a ruffled gown of apricot organdie that accentuated the black silkiness of her hair which lay off her low forehead in little soft rings.

"Thank you." Ronny modified the crispness of her tone a trifle. "We shall not care to go further than Baretti's tonight. May I ask what time the restaurant closes?"

"Ten o'clock." The gray-eyed girl seemed on the point of volunteering a remark. She half-opened her lips, then closed them almost tightly as if repenting of the impulse.

With a second "Thank you" a shade cooler than the first, Ronny concluded the brief interview. The four Lookouts had walked toward the Hall door, which stood open, and there paused to wait for her. Ordinarily, Ronny would have addressed the strangers with a certain graciousness of manner which was one of her charms. She had relaxed a little from her first reserve on the strength of their apparent willingness to direct her to Baretti's. She had not missed, however, the gray-eyed girl's deliberate checking of her own purposed remark. While she forebore to place an adverse construction upon it, nevertheless it had annoyed her. Trace of a frown lingered between her dark brows as she joined the others.

"I noticed you didn't get very chummy with that pair," greeted Jerry. "Just so you located our commissary department, Baretti. He's our star of hope at present." Jerry led the way across the veranda and down the steps.

"I know the way to Baretti's, never fear," Ronny assured. "It is one square from the west wall of the campus. Just how much of a walk that means, we shall see. It may be anywhere from a quarter to three-quarters of a mile to the west wall. We turn to our right as we go through the gateway."

"We will have to walk it, even if it is a mile," decreed Muriel. "I'd walk two miles for something to eat. I am about as hungry as I can ever remember of being. Our introduction to Hamilton! *Good night!*"

"I can't get it through my head that we are actually students at Hamilton College," declared Muriel. "I feel more as though I had just arrived at a summer hotel where people came and went without the slightest interest in one another."

"It is missing dinner at the Hall that makes it seem so. If we had had a fair chance at the dining room we would have felt more——" Jerry paused to choose a word descriptive of their united feelings. "Well, we would have felt cinched to Hamilton. That nice Miss Trent helped us, of course, but she faded away and disappeared the minute she turned us over to Miss Remson. I don't believe we can be, what you might call, fascinating. No one seems to care to linger near us. Wouldn't that be a splendid title for one of those silly old popular songs? 'No one cares to linger near,' as sung by

the great always off the key vocalist, Jerry Macy.
Wh-ir-r! Bu-z-z-z! What has happened to you
swe-e-etart, that you do not linger near-r-r? I am
lonele-e-e——"

Jerry's imitation of a phonograph rendering a
popular song of her own impromptu composition
ended suddenly. Muriel placed a defensive hand
over the singer's mouth. "Have mercy on us, Jeremiah," she begged. "You are at Hamilton now.
Try to act like some one. That's the advice I
heard one of the mill women give her unruly son
at the nursery one day last winter."

"I trust no one but ourselves heard you," was
Veronica's uncomplimentary addition, delivered in
a tone of shocked disapproval.

"I don't blame anyone for not caring to linger
near such awful sounds." Lucy's criticism, spoken
in her precise manner, produced a burst of low-
keyed laughter. It appeared to amuse Jerry most
of all.

By this time they had passed through the gateway, flanked by high, ornamental stone posts, and
were following a fairly wide, beaten footpath that
shone white in the light shed by the rising moon.
On their right hand side, the college wall of matched
gray stone rose considerably above their heads.

"This wall must be at least ten feet high and
about three or four thick." Jerry calculatingly

appraised the wall. It extends the whole way
around the campus, so far as I could tell by daylight. I was noticing it as we came into the grounds
today."

"We are not so far from the end of it now."
Marjorie made the announcement with a faint
breath of relief. "You can see the corner post
from here. I think it about a quarter of a mile
from the gate."

"And only a square from it lies our dinner, thank
goodness! Let's run." Muriel made a pretended
dash forward and was promptly checked by Jerry.
"You wouldn't let me sing. Now you need a
clamp. I'll give you a piece of advice I heard last
winter at that same old nursery: 'Walk pretty.
Don't be runnin' yourse'f all over the place.'"

"There is Baretti's across the road." Marjorie
pointed down the road a little, to where, on the
opposite side, two posts, topped by cluster electric
lights, rose on each side of a fairly wide stone walk
that was the approach to the restaurant. It stood
fully a hundred feet from the highway, an odd, one-
story structure of brown stone, looking like an inn
of a bygone period. In sharp contrast to the white
radiance of the guide lights at the end of the walk,
the light over the doorway was faint and yellow,
proceeding from a single lamp, set in a curious

wrought-iron frame, which depended from a bell-like hood over the door.

Through the narrow-paned windows streamed the welcome glow of light within. It warmed the hearts of the Five Travelers even as in departed days it had gladdened the eyes of weary wayfarers in search of purchased hospitality.

"What an odd old place!" Lucy Warner cried out in admiration. "It is like the ancient hostleries one reads of. I wonder if it has always been an inn. It must be considerably over a hundred years old."

"I suppose it is. A good deal of the country around here is historic, I believe. You remember the bulletin said Brooke Hamilton was a young man at the time of La Fayette's visit to America. That was in 1824. He and La Fayette met and the Marquis was so delighted with him that he invited him to join his suite of friends during his tour of the country. I wish it had said more about both of them, but it didn't," finished Marjorie regretfully.

"Perhaps the old Marquis de la Fayette and young Brooke Hamilton walked down the very road we walked tonight and supped at the same old inn," Veronica said, as they approached the two wide, low steps that formed the entrance to the restaurant.

"Quite likely they did," agreed Jerry. The foremost of the party, she opened the heavy, paneled door of solid oak.

A faint, united breath of approbation rose from the visitors as they stepped into a room of noble proportions. It was almost square and as beautiful an apartment as the girls had ever seen. Beam ceiling, wainscoting and floor were all of precisely the same shade and quality of dark oak. So perfectly did every foot of wood in the room match that it might have all come from one giant tree, hewn out and polished by gnomes. There was something about its perfection that suggested a castle hall of fairy lore. On each side of the room were three high-backed, massive oak benches. The tops of these were decorated by a carved oak leaf pattern, the simplicity of which was the design of genius itself. The heavy, claw-legged oak tables, oval in shape and ten in number, all bore the same pattern, carved in the table top at about two inches from the edge. There was no attempt at placing the tables in rows. They stood at intervals far enough apart to permit easy passage in and out among them. Yet each table seemed fitted into its own proper space. Moved two inches out of it, the whole scheme of artistic regularity would have been spoiled.

"It's evident that Signor Baretti never furnished this room," commented Ronny in a voice just above a whisper. "I never saw anything like it, before! never! Lead me to a seat at one of those beautiful tables."

"Yes; do let us sit down as soon as we can," echoed Muriel eagerly. "I am dying to look and look and look at everything in this adorable old room. I am glad it is almost empty. We can sit and stare and no one will be here to resent it."

This time it was Muriel who took the lead and made a bee-line for a table at the far end of the room on the right. The others followed her, quickly slipping into the oak chairs, each with its spade-shaped, high back and fairly broad seat. That these chairs were built for comfort as well as ornament the Lookouts soon discovered.

"Oh, the joy of this comfy chair," sighed Ronny. "It actually fits my back. That's more than I can say of those train seats. I am going to turn in the minute I am back at Wayland House. I am *so* tired, and a little bit sleepy."

Marjorie and Ronny shared one menu, while each of the others had one to herself. After the usual amount of comment and consultation, all decided upon consommé, roast chicken, potatoes au gratin, and a salad, with dessert and coffee to follow. Their order given to a round-faced, olive-tinted Italian girl, the Five Travelers were free to look about them for a little.

Directly across from them at a table which formed a wide obtuse angle with theirs were four girls. While the quartette had appeared to be occupied in eating ices on the entrance into the restaurant of the Sanford party, no move of the strangers had been lost on them. Four pairs of young eyes covertly appraised the newcomers. That the Five Travelers interested the other girls was clearly proven by the frequency of their glances, discreetly veiled. Deep in the exploration of the menu, the Sanford quintette were unaware that they had attracted any special attention from the diners at the one other occupied table in the room. Nevertheless, while they were busy with the ordering of their dinner, they were being subjected to a most critical survey.

By the time the consommé was served, the other group had finished the eating of their ices and risen to depart. As they left the table Marjorie glanced impersonally toward them. A sudden wave of color deepened the pink in her cheeks as she encountered four pairs of unfamiliar eyes all fastened on her. Immediately she looked away, annoyed with herself, rather than them for staring. Nor had she gained a definite idea of the appearance of any one of them, so keen was her own momentary discomfiture.

Regarding herself and her chums, the departing

diners had a very clear idea. Hardly had they stepped outside the restaurant when a low buzz of conversation began.

"Leila Harper, did you ever see anyone lovelier than that brown-eyed freshie?" inquired one of the quartette, a tall, stately girl with pale gold hair and a rather thin, interesting face. "The one in dark blue, I mean."

"No; I see a certain someone's finish, don't you?" The girl who made the reply smiled as though signally amused. In the light cast by the powerful post lights, the faces of her companions reflected that amused smile. "I could have shrieked for joy when that crowd of freshmen walked in with Beauty in their midst," she continued. "They were all very pretty girls, Selma. I really think we ought to take up the matter and have some fun over it."

"Incidentally, it would pull someone off a pedestal where she never truly belonged. I never considered Natalie Wyman a *real* beauty. She is pretty, but rather artificial, I think." The author of this criticism was an attractive young woman with wavy chestnut hair and deep blue eyes, the beauty of which was partly obscured by eye-glasses.

"I don't admire Miss Weyman's style of good looks, either, Nella." This from the fourth member of the party, a small girl with pale brown hair, pale blue eyes, with very dark brows and lashes, and a skin dazzlingly white. Standing five feet one in high heels, Vera Mason was noticeable for her doll-like daintiness of form and feature. She was not beautiful, so far as regularity of feature went, for her small nose turned up a trifle and her mouth was too wide to be classically perfect. She was, however, singularly charming.

"I had rather call you a beauty any time than apply it to her, Midget," was Leila Harper's quick return. Her eyes of true Irish blue twinkled as she said this. Suddenly she threw back her head and laughed aloud, showing white even teeth, their very soundness matching the rest of her strong-featured face and blue-black hair. Leila was of old Irish stock and very proud of it.

"Oh, girls, I have it; a plan I mean!" she exclaimed. "Now listen to the wise Irish woman and you'll agree with me that there's nothing that could fit the occasion more nearly than what I have in mind. It will do wonders in the way of curing Nat Weyman's swelled head and no one can possibly say it isn't fair."

Four abreast in the moonlight, the sophomores who had so heartily admired Marjorie strolled back to the campus, listening as they went to a plan

Leila was unfolding which appeared to afford them much anticipatory delight.

Meanwhile at the quaint old inn the Five Travelers were hungrily disposing of a comforting meal, wholly unconscious of being already a subject for discussion among a certain group of sophomores. It was as well for Marjorie's peace of mind that she did not know she had already been acclaimed a beauty at Hamilton College. Neither could the four sophomores, who were thoughtlessly planning the merited discomfiture of one girl through the raising up of another, know what a difference the carrying out of that plan would make in Marjorie Dean's life at Hamilton College.

CHAPTER XIV.

A SILENT DECLARATION OF HOSTILITY.

Not very long after the Five Travelers returned to Wayland Hall the half-past ten o'clock bell sounded. Desirous of complying with the rules of the college from the start, they had prepared for sleep in much greater haste than usual, a proceeding which Veronica deplored most of all. Accustomed to making leisurely preparations for retiring, she had known beforehand that this would be her chief annoyance when at college.

For fully twenty-five minutes after the penetrating clang of the house bell had ceased, sound of voices and light footsteps in the hall indicated that a few students, at least, were not taking the ten-thirty rule very seriously.

"What was that?" Jerry, who had dropped to sleep almost on the instant her head had found the pillow, started up in the darkness, awakened by the sharp slam of a door further down the hall.

"Oh, someone slammed a door," Marjorie replied sleepily. "I was almost asleep, but not quite. It startled me, too. There seems to be very little attention paid to the retiring bell in this house. I've heard the girls talking and laughing in the halls ever since it rang. It's quieter now. I imagine next week it will be different. College doesn't really open until Monday, you know."

"Busy Buzzy doesn't look as though she would stand for much noise. She'll begin laying down the law about next week. I hope whoever slammed that door hasn't the habit. Well, what now!"

From somewhere out on the campus the musical rhythm of chimes had begun. They played the quarter, the half, the three-quarters of the hour, then sweetly and clearly the stroke of eleven followed. Listening to it, Marjorie felt a strange new

peace of mind steal over her. Longellow's understanding lines:

"The night shall be filled with music,
    And the cares that infest the day,
Shall fold their tents like the Arabs,
    And silently steal away."

The silvery tones had a vastly soothing effect
upon her troubled spirit. Altogether, it had been
one of the most dispiriting days she had ever lived.
She now hailed the ringing of the chimes as a kind
of lullaby to her cares. Here was a second friend
of whom she was sure she could never grow tired.

"That's eleven o'clock. Didn't those chimes
sound pretty? I suppose that's the end of the limit
bell here at Hamilton. If you aren't in bed when
the chimes play eleven, you are a disgrace to your
Alma Mater. If you aren't asleep by that time,
well—you can hear 'em. I've heard them, I'm
going to sleep this minute. Night, Sweet Marjoram."

"Good night, Jeremiah." Marjorie lay awake for
a little, her thoughts on her father and mother.
She knew that they were thinking of her and a
sense of soothing warmth enfolded her, born of the
knowledge of their steadfast adoration.

Marjorie awakened next morning to find the sun
in her eyes and herself not quite certain of where

she was. She glanced across the room to where Jerry's couch was situated. It was without an occupant. "Oh!" she exclaimed in consternation. Her eyes hastily sought the mission wall clock. It was only ten minutes to seven. Reassured, she lay still and viewed the room by broad daylight. The furnishings were pretty and comfortable. The color scheme of the room was delft blue. The walls were papered in a white mica-stripe with a plain white ceiling. A wide, ragged border of bachelor's buttons added vastly to the dainty effect. The two wash-stands, chiffoniers and dressing tables had Japanese covers of white stamped in blue figures. The hard-wood floor was covered by a velvet rug in three shades of blue, and the couch covers were also in indeterminate blues. There were two easy chairs, one willow rocker and two straight cane-seated chairs. A good sized library table occupied the center of the room. It was of black walnut and an antique. At each end of the room was a door opening into a closet, large enough to permit the hanging of wearing apparel without crowding. All the necessary effects having been provided, it remained to the occupants to supply their own individual decorations.

The entrance into the room of Jerry, her round face rosy from her morning scrub, brought Marjorie's inspection of her now "house" to an end.

"I've been looking at our new room ever since I woke up," saluted Marjorie. "It is pretty, I think. I am not used to blue, though. It matches you better than me, Jerry."

"Yes, I see it does. It's large enough for the furniture, without crowding. That's what I like about it. I believe——"

The silver-tongued chimes cut into Jerry's speech, ringing out a live little prelude before striking seven. Came the striking of the hour, a slow, measured salute to the sunny autumn morning.

"You may politely say 'excuse me,' next time you butt into my conversation." Jerry nodded an admonishing head in the direction from whence the musical sounds had come. "Funny I didn't hear those chimes at six o'clock. I was awake."

"Maybe they don't play them every hour," suggested Marjorie. "I remember when we were living in B—— an Episcopal Church near where we lived had a set of chimes installed. They started out by having them played every hour. It annoyed the nearby residents so much that they finally rang them only at six o'clock in the evening and on special occasions. They never bothered General and Captain and me. We were sorry to lose them. It was like meeting some one I hadn't heard of in a long while to hear those good old bells last night. There are two things I love already about Hamilton. One is the campus; the other is the chimes."

"I agree with you about the campus. I don't know yet about the chimes. Familiarity with them may breed anything but admiration." Jerry was only jesting. Such was her nature that she shied at the proximity of sentiment. She had it in her to be sure, but she kept it hidden far beneath the surface.

"You had better hurry along to your bath," she now advised. "By half-past seven the lavatory will become suddenly very popular."

"I'm going this minute." Marjorie had already donned a negligee and was hastily thrusting her feet into quilted satin slippers.

As she stepped from her room into the hall, a door on the opposite side, above the room occupied by Lucy and Ronny, swung open with a jerk. On the threshold appeared Natalie Weyman. She was evidently in a bad humor, for her heavy brows were sharply drawn in an ugly scowl. Her eyes happening to light on Marjorie, her face grew perceptibly darker. With a smothered exclamation, she disappeared into her room again, banging the door. She had not even attempted a "good morning," but had stared at Marjorie as though she had never seen her before.

Not in the least impressed, Marjorie continued imperturbably toward the lavatory. She had made two discoveries, however. She knew now who had slammed the door on the previous night. She knew, too, that Natalie Weyman had no real feeling of friendliness toward her. She had heard enough from the three callers of the evening before to arraign them in her mind as leaning very hard toward snobbishness. If they were snobs, she wished to keep far away from them. Further, she had no intention of regarding Miss Weyman's call as anything but a duty-prompted affair. Not one of the three young women had extended an informal invitation to the Five Travelers to visit them in their rooms. If the select Sans Soucians expected to see herself and chums go out of their way to please, they would be disappointed.

CHAPTER XV.

THE GIRLS OF WAYLAND HALL.

In the lavatory she encountered the two students of whom Ronny had made inquiry regarding Baretti's. The black-haired girl looked at her, then nodded pleasantly. Marjorie returned the salutation with a half-shy smile which the square-chinned, sandy-haired girl shrewdly noted. Regarding Marjorie intently for an instant, very deliberately she stretched forth a hand.

"Good morning," she said, in a rather deep voice for a girl. "Did you have any trouble finding Baretti's?"

"Not a bit, thank you." This time Marjorie's smile broke forth in all its sunny beauty. "We might have lost our way if we had not met you. We saw some girls in the rustic house as we left the Hall, but we met no others. If we had tried to find it ourselves, and turned to the left instead of the right, I don't know where we would have landed."

"Not anywhere near food; I can tell you that." It was the tall girl's turn to smile. Marjorie liked her instantly. She admired her capable chin and direct, honest expression. "You would have gone rambling along toward the Hamilton Estates."

"We saw them yesterday as we drove to the college from the station. They are so artistically laid out. I am anxious to see Hamilton Arms. I have been interested in what the bulletin says of Brooke Hamilton. We loved Baretti's. It must have been an inn, long ago. That is what we thought."

"It was," answered the brunette. She now offered her hand. "It used to be called 'Comfort Inn.' You and your friends are freshmen, I know. Miss Remson told us that there were to be five

freshmen from the same town at the Hall this year.
You see the Hall was fairly well filled last June
with prospective sophs and a few juniors and
seniors. I think only two other freshmen besides
yourselves were able to get in here, this year. We
mustn't keep you standing here. I am Martha Merrick, and this is my pal, Rosalind Black. We are
sophomores. We are not so very much inflated
over our high estate. You may look at us, of
course, and even speak to us."

"I will try not to overstep bounds," Marjorie
promised. "I am Marjorie Dean, and I am glad
to meet you. I haven't yet learned a freshman's
prerogatives. I must rely upon my high and
mighty sophomore sisters to enlighten me."

"We will, never fear. You may expect to see us
in your room before long; perhaps this evening, if
you are not busy."

"You will be welcome. We have nothing special
to do this evening. We shall look forward to seeing
you, and treat you with proper respect, you may be
sure."

All three laughed merrily at Marjorie's assurance. The two sophomores then left her to her
morning ablutions.

" 'The sweetest flower that grows' " sang Martha Merrick softly, the minute the door closed
between them and Marjorie.

"Isn't she, though," quietly agreed her companion. "She isn't a snob, Martha. She has gentle manners."

"Oh, I know it! What a relief to see a beauty who isn't wrapped up in herself. Did you ever see anything more gorgeous than that head of brown curls. If I wished to be further poetical I could quote numerous lines that would apply to her."

"She is lovely enough to inspire them, but she is more than that. She is a very fine girl. Depend upon it, Martha, her friends are worth knowing or they wouldn't be her friends. That's the way I read our stunning freshie. I hope I am right. A few staunch democratics besides ourselves and Nella and Leila are needed here to offset Millionaire Row."

Meanwhile Marjorie was luxuriating in her morning scrub, a happy little smile playing about her lips. It was so cheering to meet friendliness at last. Miss Merrick and Miss Black were far more according to her college ideals. Before she had completed her toilet several girls dropped into the lavatory. Long before this, her curls had been fastened up, close to her head. Nevertheless the strangers stared more or less politely at her. Two of them she thought she recognized as among the four she had seen at Baretti's.

About to leave the lavatory, one of the towels

on her arm slid to the floor as she essayed to open the door. Some one behind her recovered it and handed it to her. Turning to thank the doer of the courtesy, she caught a flash of white teeth and the steady regard of two bright blue eyes. This was Marjorie's first impression of Leila Harper.

"I am ever so much obliged to you," she said.

"You are welcome." The other girl betrayed no special interest in Marjorie. Nevertheless Leila Harper was interested to the point of deliberately endeavoring to draw her into conversation. About to turn away, Leila spoke again. "I believe I saw you last night at Baretti's."

"I thought I recognized you as one of the students who sat at a table on the right," Marjorie instantly replied. Not a word more did she volunteer. Instinctively she recognized a difference in the stranger's manner from that of the two students with whom she had recently talked.

"Baretti's is a quaint old place, is it not?" remarked the other, a shade more cordially.

"We admired it. We were too late for dinner at the Hall last night, so we were directed there." Marjorie could not bring herself to be too casual.

"It's a good place to eat when you have a brand new check from home in your pocket. Toward the last of the month I am generally to be found at the Hall at meal-time." Her blue eyes twinkled in true

Irish fashion and her white teeth again flashed into
evidence.

"I suppose it will be the same with me before I
have been here long. At home my chums and I
used to part with our pocket money at a tea-room
called Sargent's. Now we shall undoubtedly do
our best to make Baretti rich."

"Where do you come from?" The question was
asked with abrupt directness.

Marjorie answered in quietly even tones, adding
a few more explanatory sentences concerning herself and chums. It had occurred to her that this
latest acquaintance had engaged in conversation
with her for a purpose of her own. Realizing that
time was on the wing, and Jerry probably impatient
at her non-return, she excused herself and pattered
down the hall to her room.

"I thought you would never come back," greeted
Jerry. "Have you seen the girls?"

"No; not one of them. I met those two girls
who directed us to Baretti's last night. They are
sophomores. I like them. Miss Remson mentioned
us to them.

"Now I told you Busy Buzzy was on the job all
the time. She ought to be our press agent. Only
we don't need one. True worth will always be discovered, sooner or later. Who else knows our

home town and past history as given out by our
little Buzz-about?"

"No one else, so far as I know." Marjorie was
forced to smile at Jerry's nonsense. She did not
altogether approve of Busy Buzzy and Buzz-about
as names for the odd little manager. She doubted
if Miss Remson would hail either with joy. "I met
another girl, too. One of those we saw at Baretti's
last night." Marjorie briefly described her and the
circumstances of the meeting.

"Yes; I remember her. I took a good look at
those four. They were watching us, too. They
were very clever about it, though."

Marjorie said nothing for a little. Engaged with
her hair at the dressing table, a decided frown
shadowed her forehead.

"What's the matter?" Seated where she could
see her chum's face in the mirror, Jerry had instantly noted the shadow.

"Oh, nothing much. It seemed to me this girl
didn't care about being friendly. She acted more
as if she were trying to find out what sort of person I was. It wasn't what she said to me, but her
manner that made me think it. I felt toward her as
I might have toward a stranger I had chanced to
meet somewhere in public and exchanged courtesies
with."

"She was probably trying to find out your principles and so forth. She may be either a snob or a snob-hater. It wouldn't surprise me if that were the main issue here," was Jerry's shrewd guess. "In either case she would be anxious to know how to class you. According to Miss Archer's friend, Miss Hutchison, the snob proposition has become a grand nuisance here. Who knows? Before long we may be taking part in a regular fight against 'our crowd.' Maybe both sides are looking for freshman recruits."

"Well, if it's a fight based on money, you and Ronny are eligible to 'our crowd,' retorted Marjorie mischievously. "The rest of us can't qualify."

"It's a good thing," Jerry said sarcastically. "Any time you catch me toddling along with that foolish aggregation you may discard me forever."

The measured raps on the door turned the attention of both girls to it. Jerry answered it, admitting Muriel.

"Top of the morning," she saluted. "Ready to go down to breakfast? Have you seen Ronny and Lucy yet?"

"I am ready and Marjorie soon will be. No; the girls haven't appeared. We have loads of time for breakfast this morning. No danger of getting left."

Muriel at once began to recount her meeting in the lavatory with two freshmen. She was in the

midst of it when more rapping announced Ronny
and Lucy.

"I was afraid you had gone down stairs," were
Ronny's first words. "I slept until the last minute
as usual. Lucy was up long before me. She set
off for the lavatory, bold as you please. When she
opened the door and saw half a dozen strangers,
she took fright and hustled back to our room. Then
she sat around like a goose until I woke up."

Lucy merely smiled a little at this exposé. "I
needed Ronny's moral support," she said whimsi-
cally. "Afterward I was sorry I didn't brave it
out. The second time the lavatory held twice as
many girls."

"We landed in the middle of 'our crowd,'" reported Veronica, looking extremely bored. "They
paid no attention to us, for which I was duly thankful. Like myself, I suppose they hate to get up
early. I didn't mind it at home, for I can take my
time. I often get up at five o'clock when Father
and I are going for a long ride over the ranch.
But to rise early, then have to hurry!" Ronny made
a gesture eloquent of disfavor.

"Miss Weyman said there were eighteen girls in
their sorority," interposed Jerry. "I wonder how
many of them room in this house?"

"A dozen at least; perhaps the whole eighteen,"
replied Ronny. "There were eight or nine of them

in the lavatory. I heard them asking where Florence and Lita were, so I daresay they are among the elect. Miss Weyman wasn't there nor Miss Cairns. I saw and heard Miss Vale, she was talking at the top of her lungs."

"Did that Miss Vale speak to you?" Jerry questioned abruptly.

"I happened to catch her eye and she gave me a wee little nod and a sickly smile," Ronny answered, in satirical amusement.

"Marjorie and I have an inkling that there are two factions at the Hall. If that's the case— Good-bye to a peaceful college life," predicted Jerry. "While we may think we can keep clear of both factions, we can never do it. Mark my words, within six weeks from now we'll be all out of patience with 'our crowd.' Then look out for fireworks."

CHAPTER XVI.

CULTIVATING CLASS SPIRIT.

FOLLOWING Jerry's ominous prophecy, nothing of any special moment occurred to mar the Five Travelers' peace of mind during their first week at Hamilton. So occupied were they in choosing their subjects, arranging their recitation periods and adapting themselves to the new life that they paid small attention to the comings and goings of the coterie of millionaire's purse-proud daughters which Wayland Hall housed.

The Sans Soucians were deep in a round of sociabilities, to which it appeared that only a few juniors and seniors were eligible. To the other girls of the sophomore class, they accorded a cool shoulder. A handful of moneyed freshmen found favor with them and were therefore made much of. The Lookouts, however, were not among these. They had been privately rated by their quondam callers as plebians and dropped.

While Marjorie and Muriel had chosen the classical course, Lucy and Jerry had decided on the scientific and Ronny on the philosophical. As they had arrived at Hamilton three days before the official opening of the college, they had plenty of time to discuss together the respective merits of their chosen courses and arrange satisfactorily their recitation periods.

The making of these necessary arrangements, together with unpacking their trunks and attention to the countless details relative to their physical comfort, left them little time during those first busy days for social amenities outside their own intimate circle.

With Helen Trent, Martha Merrick and Rosalind

Black they had become fairly friendly. Helen, in particular, had already become a welcome visitor to their rooms. She had a habit of dropping in on one or another of them with a bit of lively, but harmless, college gossip, that was infinitely divert‐ ing. She never prolonged her visits to the weari‐ some point. She was never in the way. In fact, she was usually in a hurry. The difficulty lay in trying to hold her, never in wishing for her to depart.

Thanks to Miss Remson, the five girls had been given places at one table in the dining room. At meal time they were, therefore, a close corporation. Muriel's acquaintance with the two freshmen, Mary Cornell and Eva Ingram, both from New York City, had flourished to the extent that they had made her one evening call which she had returned. Like herself, they had made no acquaintances out‐ side the Hall since their arrival and relied on each other for company.

Toward the end of the Sanford girls' second week at Hamilton a number of things happened. First of all, Muriel acquired a room-mate as a result of persistent "buzzing" on the part of the manager. When first asked to share her room with the dissat‐ isfied junior, Miss Barlow, Muriel had thought it over and decided in the negative. Miss Barlow was not to be thus easily balked of her desire. She persisted with Miss Remson and Miss Remson persisted with Muriel until the latter finally revoked her earlier refusal.

"Anything to have the subject off my mind," she confided to her chums. "I'm tired of being waylaid by Miss Remson. I don't blame Jeremiah for calling her Busy Buzzy. Just wait until you see my room-mate! Her name is Hortense. It ought to be Moretense. She is the stiffest person I ever saw. She walks as though she were wired and then starched for the occasion. I had a lovely conversation with her last night. She moved in after classes yesterday. I talked quite a lot. All she said was 'Yes,' 'Do you?' and 'I believe not.' "

The name "Moretense" found instant favor with Jerry, while the other three Lookouts had hard work to keep their faces straight when they chanced to encounter dignified Miss Barlow about the Hall. Very tall and straight to rigidity, her set features never seemed to relax. Even an abundant head of blue black hair, loosely coiffed, did not serve to soften the wax-like immobility of her rather broad face. Whether her disposition and temperament matched her peculiar physical presence was something Muriel had not had time to fathom.

Muriel's room-mate, nevertheless, was of more interest to the Five Travelers than the notice of the class election which was to take place at the beginning of their third week at Hamilton. They had long since learned that the majority of the freshmen had made harbor at Acasia House and Silverton Hall, both noted as freshmen domiciles. Recitations had familiarized them with the other members of their class, which was a small one for Hamilton, numbering only eighty-two students. Still they had not become much acquainted with their classmates and they had not yet reached a stage of active inter-est in their class.

Summoned to election one windy Tuesday afternoon, following recitations, the Lookouts began to experience the beginning of class enthusiasm. The majority of 19— were bright-faced, bright-eyed girls who reminded Marjorie of her class at Sanford High. It was seeing them together that brought to her a tardy realization that she had been too entirely wrapped up in her own affairs to cultivate a proper class spirit. Had she entered Hamilton College alone, she would have made acquaintances in her class more quickly. Surrounded by four of her intimate friends, her hours of leisure were always spent with them. Of the five girls, she had the peculiar personality which invites friendship. Muriel came next in this, Ronny was not interested in acquiring new friends. Jerry was hard to please, and Lucy was too reserved. A large number of freshmen at Wayland Hall would have also made a difference. As this was not the case, the Lookouts were obliged to admit among themselves that they had been lacking in class spirit.

The freshmen from Silverton Hall, about thirty in number, were, to all appearances, taking the lead in the class election. Three of the candidates nominated for office who won, respectively, the presidency, vice-presidency and secretaryship were from there. As the candidates were obliged to come up to the front of Science Hall where the meeting was held, the Lookouts had at least the opportunity to see the nominees and judge their fitness, as nearly as they could, from their personal appearance. All five approved in particular the new president, Miss Graham, a fair-haired, pink-cheeked young woman with sparkling brown eyes and a ready, sunshiny smile.

The treasurer-elect was an Acasia House girl, while the various committees were about equally divided between the two houses. While the Lookouts were entirely satisfied with the result of the election, they felt, nevertheless, a trifle out of things. They had had no part in the merry electioneering which had evidently gone on under their very noses. More, it appeared that another class meeting had been held before this, of which they had seen no notice on the Hall bulletin board, neither had they received a written or verbal summons to it.

During a recess after the election granted for the purpose of shaking hands with the officers, Marjorie found the golden brown eyes of the president fixed very kindly on her.

"You are at Wayland Hall, aren't you? I know you are Miss Dean, for I saw you on the campus over two weeks ago and made inquiry about you. It is too bad we don't have any of the same recitation periods. I would have met you before this. I thought you would be at our other class meeting, but neither you nor your four friends came. I haven't time to talk any more now. Observe that line of congratulators. After the meeting, if you will wait for me, several of the Silverton girls would like to meet you and your friends."

"Of course we will wait, and feel highly honored." Marjorie flashed the president a winsome smile, albeit she was nonplussed as to why pretty Miss Graham had been so anxious to meet her, in particular. She was also bent on learning more of the other class meeting from which they had in some strange manner been cut out.

The meeting over, the Sanford quintette stood off to one side, waiting for Miss Graham. She presently came up to them, accompanied by half a dozen freshmen, evidently close friends of hers.

An introducing session ensued, punctuated by laughter and gay pleasantries. It produced a more comforting effect on the Five Travelers than had anything since the day when Helen Trent, by her kindly manner, had taken the strain off their arrival.

"What do you think of that, girls? Miss Dean and her friends did not know a *thing* about the other class meeting we held here! We sent notices to all the campus houses, requesting them bulletined. There was a notice on the big bulletin board, too. The one outside Hamilton Hall, you know."

"Why, Portia, don't you remember? It was awfully windy that day and some one came into the Hall and said that there wasn't a sign of our notice on the large board. It must have blown away. That was at noon. We were to put out another and I believe it was forgotten." This information came from a small girl with very wide-open gray eyes and brown hair, cropped close to her head. She had the face of a mischievous, small boy.

"Yes, Robin, I do recall it, now that you have reminded me. Much obliged. That explains, perhaps, why you did not see it on the main bulletin board. It seems strange that the notice we sent to Wayland Hall was not posted there. Miss Remson, I understand, is always particularly careful to post the notices sent her."

"If Miss Remson received it, she would not fail to post it," asserted Marjorie. "Was it mailed or delivered by a freshman messenger?"

"I took it to Wayland Hall." It was the girl Miss Graham addressed as Robin who answered. "I handed it to a maid in a sealed envelope, addressed to Miss Remson."

"Perhaps some of the sophs saw it on the bulletin board and nabbed it for a joke," suggested a tall, handsome brunette who had been introduced to the Lookouts as Miss Scott.

"A poor sort of joke, I should say," Robina Page said, a trifle contemptuously.

"Well, we were told we might expect——" Blanche Scott broke off short, with a significant twitch of compressed lips.

"It was unfortunate, of course," Portia Graham hastily remarked, "but we'll hope no more notices go astray. You freshmen at the Hall had better keep in closer touch with us. That means come over to our house and be sociable. How many more freshmen besides yourselves live at Wayland Hall?"

"Two; Miss Cornell and Miss Ingram." Muriel supplied this information. "They were sitting toward the back of the hall when the meeting began. There they are!" She located the two at a short distance from them, talking earnestly to the student who had been elected to the vice-presidency. She bore a slight resemblance to Irma Linton. The Lookouts often saw her on the campus and during recitation periods, but did not know her name.

"Oh; I see them. They are in good hands." Miss Graham looked relieved. "Elaine Hunter is the sweetest girl in the whole world, I believe. Just to be in the same house with her is to love her."

"She reminds us of a friend of ours at home." Jerry glanced very approvingly toward the pretty, freshman. "We have noticed her on the campus. If she is as fine as Irma Linton, our friend, she is worth knowing. We were sorry that Irma didn't choose Hamilton, but her mother was a Wellesley graduate and anxious for Irma to enter Wellesley."

"I know how that goes," nodded Miss Graham. "My dearest friend was packed off to Smith College to please her family. She didn't care to enter Smith, but went as a matter of duty."

At this juncture, Elaine Hunter, accompanied by Miss Cornell and Miss Ingram, joined the group around the president and more introducing followed. Presently the whole party trooped out of Science Hall and across the wide campus together, making the still autumn dusk ring with their clear young voices.

From the Silverton Hall girls the Lookouts

learned that the regular freshman dance, which the sophomores gave each year to their younger sisters, was soon to take place. The date had not yet been given out. It was the autumn event at Hamilton. The juniors and seniors could come to it if they chose. On St. Valentine's night the juniors always gave a masquerade to all three of the other classes. Washington's birthday the seniors claimed as theirs and gave either a play or a costume dance. To the freshmen belonged the Apple Blossom hop, a dance given by them each spring in the time of apple blossoms.

When the seven freshmen bade their congenial classmates good-bye, and struck off across the campus for Wayland Hall, it was with a new and delightful sense of fellowship and cheer. Like the Lookouts, the two girls from New York City had been disappointed at the lack of cordiality they had met with at Hamilton. Neither had known of the first class meeting until after it had been held, and both were a trifle hurt at having been ignored. As the Lookouts had known nothing at all about it, they at least could not be blamed for not having passed word of it along.

"Well, we are at last beginning to meet the folks," Jerry said with a certain touch of grim satisfaction, as the five girls settled themselves in Ronny's and Lucy's room for a few moment's private chat before the dinner bell sounded.

"If we were living at Silverton Hall or Acasia House we would be far more in touch with college matters," commented Ronny reflectively.

"You may blame me for choosing Wayland Hall," Marjorie reminded. "I liked the picture of it better than the others."

"Yes; you picked this stately old lemon and we followed your lead." Jerry favored her room-mate with a genial grin which the latter returned in kind. "We forgive you for it. How could you guess who else beside Busy Buzzy lived here? I like the Hall. The rooms are good, the meals are gooder, and the conveniences are goodest of all. It has the prettiest lawn and veranda of them all, too."

"It's a blue-ribbon place or Moretense wouldn't have besieged Miss Remson to let her in here. I decline to say Busy Buzzy for fear of getting the habit. I am too careless to apply it to her only in privacy. I'm likely to come to grief," Muriel said lightly.

"It's no worse than 'Moretense,'" argued Jerry. You say that all the time. I hope, for your sake, you won't get caught saying *that*."

"It sounds so much like 'Hortense' that I could get away with it," retorted Muriel. "Anyway, I like to name people according to their lights and so do you. Long may we wave with no embarrassing accidents." Whereupon Jerry and Muriel solemnly shook hands.

"Isn't it time we had a meeting of the Five Travelers?" Lucy Warner broke in irrelevantly. "On the train we said we would have one once a week. This is our third week here and we haven't had even one."

"Quite true, Lucificus Warneriferous, sage and philosopher," agreed Jerry, with a gravity which would have been admirable on any other occasion.

"Jeremiah is all taken up with the naming habit," put in Ronny slyly.

"Ain't I jist," chuckled Jerry. "Our cook always says that when I ask her if she is going to the movies on Saturday night."

"We are away off the subject." Marjorie had done little but laugh since the five had sat down to talk.

"Certainly, we are." Lucy regarded Jerry with pretended severity. "We never keep to a subject when Geraldine Macy is present." Though she spoke in jest there was a curious light in Lucy's green eyes which no one present except Marjorie understood. It always appeared when Lucy was anxious to impart a confidence.

"You have something special to tell us, haven't you, Lucy?" Marjorie quietly asked.

"Yes, I have, but I wish it to be a confidence

made to the Five Travelers," Lucy said with stiff positiveness. "While what I have to tell you is not anything which touches us personally, it is something which should be brought to your attention. I don't wish to tell you until we have a meeting. I think we had better have that meeting no later than tomorrow night."

CHAPTER XVII.

A HOUSE DIVIDED AGAINST ITSELF.

THE result of Lucy's strong plea for an official meeting of the Five Travelers was a gathering, in hers and Ronny's room, on the next evening. As all had agreed to prepare for tomorrow's recitations first, it was nine o'clock when they assembled to hear what Lucy had to say.

What Marjorie said, however, the next moment after Ronny had turned the key in the door was: "Girls, I'd like to have Ronny take charge of this meeting. While there are only a handful of us, someone ought to be at the head."

Veronica demurred vigorously. She was overruled and found herself mistress of ceremonies whether she would or no.

"Very well," she at last accepted, "I will do the

best I can to be an illustrious head to this noble
organization. To begin with, I will say that I admire Lucy's policy. What we report here weekly
is official. If we merely talked it over in our rooms
it would sometimes seem like gossiping, even
though we did not intend it to be such. I don't
know that I have anything special to tell. I will
say this: Much as I like Wayland Hall and Miss
Remson, I do not like the atmosphere of it. It is
a house quietly divided against itself. There is no
unity here of the better element of girls. There
ought to be. I am ready to say how such unity
might be brought about. I am not sure that I wish
to make it my business. I am not sure that it would
come under the head of being a Lookout. As the
Five Travelers we have made no pledges, thus far,"
she concluded with her strange, flickering smile.

"While I was anxious to carry out the plan we
made on the train about the Five Travelers, what I
have to tell you really comes under the head of
being a Lookout." Lucy paused and glanced around
the uneven semi-circle into which the girls had
drawn their chairs. "Someone I know is in great
need of help, or rather protection, and that is Miss
Langly."

"In need of protection," repeated Muriel Harding,
in a surprised tone. "What awful calamity hangs
over that quiet little mouse's head?" The other

three girls also looked in mild amazement. Katherine Langly, a quiet little sophomore, was the one acquaintance Lucy had made by herself.

"It is those hateful sophomores from whom she needs protection," explained Lucy, smiling faintly at Muriel's question. "They torment her in all sorts of sly ways. I mean the ones Jerry named 'our crowd.' They wish her to leave the Hall as a friend of theirs, a freshman, is trying to get in here. You see she won a Hamilton scholarship. I mean one offered by Hamilton College. She tried special examinations made up by the Hamilton faculty of years ago. Her papers were considered so nearly perfect that she was awarded the special scholarship which no one had won for twenty years. It covers every expense. Mr. Brooke Hamilton founded it and laid aside a sum of money for it. It is still in bank. So few have won this scholarship, the money has accumulated until it is now a very large sum."

"How interesting!" the four listeners exclaimed in the same breath.

"Truly, I shall never rest until I have dug up a lot of Mr. Brooke Hamilton's history," asserted Marjorie. "He was almost as interesting as Benjamin Franklin, who was the most interesting person I ever heard of. Pardon me, Lucy. I am the one who is off the subject tonight."

"What does 'our crowd' do in the way of ragging Miss Langly?" demanded Jerry, bristling into sudden belligerence. "They make me weary! The idea of insulting a girl who has more mind in a minute than the whole bunch will have in a century."

"They never speak to her, although this is her second year at the Hall. You see, the scholarship mentions a certain room in each of four campus houses which the winner may have the use of. She cannot share it with anyone. The terms state that a young woman brilliant enough to win the scholarship has t'.e right to exclusive privacy."

"Wasn't that dear in Brooke Hamilton?" Ronny cried out involuntarily. "I adore the memory of that fine gentleman. I shall certainly join you in the history-digging job, Marjorie."

"Now let Brooke Hamilton rest," ordered Jerry. "I am the only one of you who really has a mind to the subject."

"Give me credit," emphasized Muriel. "I haven't said a word. I've listened hard. What else do these millionaires do, Lucy?" Muriel wagged her head proudly at Jerry to show the latter how closely she had been paying attention.

"Oh, they make remarks about her clothes and snub her dreadfully at table. She sits at the same table as that Miss Cairns and Miss Vale. They take turns staring steadily at her, sometimes, until they make her so nervous she can scarcely eat. She said it wasn't so bad last year for she sat at a table with Miss Harper and Miss Sherman. Besides, these girls weren't trying to get her room. It has been worse this year. One day last week Miss Myers, she is a ringleader among them, stopped her in the hall and asked her if she would not be willing to trade rooms with Miss Elster, the freshman they are working to get into the Hall. Miss Langly explained that, on account of her scholarship, she had no choice in the matter. She was angry, and she also said that if she were free to make the exchange she would not do it. Then she walked away. That evening Miss Myers reported her to Miss Remson for burning her lights late, walking noisily about her room and slamming her door after the ten-thirty bell had rung."

"Why, that is simply outrageous!" cried Marjorie, her brown eyes sparkling with indignation. "Surely, Miss Remson did not credit it."

"No; she told Miss Langly to pay no attention to it. She called her privately into her office and told her about the report soon after it had been made. She said that she had simply informed Miss Meyers that the person who slammed her door so frequently and late was Miss Weyman, not Miss Langly. That if Miss Langly burned her lights after the bell had rung it was because she had had permission to do so. That if a number of the other young women at the Hall would pattern after Miss Langly, it would save her an infinite amount of trouble."

"Good for Busy Buzzy," cheered Jerry, standing up and waving her arms.

"Less noise or some one will report us," warned Ronny laughingly. "These millionairesses will be out for our scalps when they know us a little better. I think the whole thing is shameful. It is just the way the girls at Miss Trevelyn's used to be. Only there were no poor girls there. They used to act spitefully to one another. Of course Miss Langly knows that you have told us this, Lucy?"

"Yes; I asked her if she cared if you girls knew it. I said I was sure you would fight for her. She said she did not wish you to do so, but she did not care if I told you. She supposed almost every one at the Hall knew it."

"There isn't much we can do at first," said Marjorie thoughtfully. Every pair of eyes were turned on her sweet face as she began speaking. "Our best plan is the old way we have always done; take her under our wing. There is room at our table for another plate. I will ask Miss Remson to make that change. That will help a good deal.

The rest of the time she can keep out of those girls' way."

"We ought to do a little press-agenting. I mean, tell everybody how brilliant Miss Langly is and about the scholarship," was Muriel's inspiration. "We'll start the Silverton Hall crowd to eulogizing her. If these bullies find most of the college admires her, they will be a little more careful. They aren't crazy to take a back seat. They love to be popular and have the mob follow them about."

"Lucy, you must tell Miss Langly to be sure and attend the reception. She owes it to herself to be there." This from Ronny, in decided tones.

"She said she would like to invite me," Lucy colored with shy embarrassment, "but she was afraid we would not be well-treated. So many of those girls are sophomores. She thinks they will run the reception."

"You tell *her* to go ahead and invite you," commanded Jerry. "We'll be there to stand behind you. We may not have a special escort. If not, we can go in a bunch. Has she a family, or is she an orphan, or what about her?"

"She's an orphan. She worked her way through high school. She lived with an old lady and worked for her board. She has had a very sad life."

"I am proud to know her," Ronny said simply.

"If I had known her long ago I would have helped her."

"We will make her our close friend and see what happens," planned Marjorie. "If the Sans Soucians choose to become offended with us on that account, we shall understand better how to deal with them. It may be as well to let them know our principles. They will then set us down as prigs and leave us alone."

This sentiment having been approved, Ronny inquired if there was anything else to be reported by anyone present. Nothing of an adverse nature happened to the Lookouts since the evening of their arrival, neither had anything especially pleasant occurred which they had not shared. The official confidence session was therefore closed until the next week, and the girls fell to discussing the coming dance and what they intended to wear. None of them except Lucy were likely to have a special escort, was the modest opinion.

Two days after their private conclave, the date of the dance was announced on all the bulletin boards. All freshmen were earnestly urged to be present. Followed the happiness of special invitation for all of the Lookouts. Helen Trent invited Jerry. Leila Harper invited Marjorie, greatly to the latter's amazement. Vera Mason requested the pleasure of becoming Ronny's escort. As for Muriel, she held her breath when stolid Miss Barlow made offer to become her escort on the eventful night. Muriel accepted ceremoniously and escaped from the room immediately after being invited for fear of disgracing herself by laughing. Later, Nella Sherman invited her, but Muriel had to decline, with some regret, in favor of her odd roommate.

The dance was to take place in the gymnasium on Thursday evening one week after the first announcement had been made. For three afternoons and evenings before the festivity, the majority of the sophomores were to be found in the gymnasium, following classes, industriously engaged in beautifying the spacious room for the affair. It may be said that the Sans Soucians were strictly on the scene. In fact, they endeavored to take charge. As they contributed a wealth of decorative material in the way of small velvet rugs, expensive satin and velvet cushions and velour draperies, they appeared to consider themselves of vital importance to the affair.

The laborious part of the decorating, however, they took good care to portion out to the sophomores outside their own intimate circle. Joan Myers, as president of the sophomore class, had called a special meeting and appointed a special committee on decorations for the dance. This committee comprised Leila Harper, Helen Trent, Nella Sherman, Vera Mason, Hortense Barlow, Martha Merrick and Selma Sanbourne. The Sans Soucians were generous in the extreme in contributing luxurious effects, but they were niggardly in offering to help with the hard work attending the disposal of them. They lounged about the gymnasium and criticized freely, but they did very little actual labor.

The odd part was to see the stolidity of the hardworking committee, as assisted by the willing element among the sophomores, they toiled on, paying scarcely more attention to their indolent classmates than if they had been a few ubiquitous flies. On the first afternoon of the three preceding the hop, the committee hired a light wagon and went to the Hamilton Forest, a piece of woods situated about two miles south of the college. They returned at dusk laden with the fragrant spoils of the woods. On the second afternoon and evening the work of transforming the gymnasium into an autumn bower was skilfully performed. A creditable number of juniors and seniors did diligent service on this hard detail. On the third afternoon they arranged the cushions, draperies, chairs and like effects. Fortunately for them the Sans were absent. They were bending their valuable energies toward beautifying themselves for the evening.

The Sans Soucians numbered eighteen sopho-

mores, but their sympathizers numbered as many
more. In a class of ninety-two, at least twenty
took small interest in class matters. This left a
trifle less than half of the class to uphold democracy. As freshmen, the nobler element of girls had
made some effort to stem the rising tide of snobbishness in their class. Utterly disgusted, they had at
length, quietly withdrawn from association with an
unworthy enemy. Now at the beginning of their
sophomore year, indications marked no change for
the better.

"Well, sophies, the job is done, and be-utifu!ly
done!" sang out Leila Harper. Unfastening the
voluminous blue bungalow apron she had worn
while at work, she whipped it off and stood survey-
ing her scratched and dusty hands.

"The whole thing is a positive dream!" admired
Vera Mason, clasping her small hands. "I can't
help saying the gym looks much finer than last
year."

"You may say it. Don't let the junies hear you."
Leila's voice carried the peculiar inflection that
marks the Celt the world over. "It remains to be
seen who will claim the credit," she added with a
touch of satire. "Never mind, wait until the evening is over. There will be a grand surprise for
some folks." She laughed softly, in anticipatory
enjoyment of the surprise she was predicting. "I

must hurry along.   Remember, I am to escort Beauty to the hop."

"Do try to be on time, Leila," counseled Selma Sanbourne.   "You're always late, you know."

"That I am, Swede," retorted Leila, in good-humored agreement.

While Vera Mason rejoiced in the nickname "Midget," Selma, being a Scandinavian,had received that of "Swede."   She occasionally retaliated by call-ing Leila "Ireland," the latter having been the one to apply the two aforesaid nicknames to her chums.

"Don't be disappointed if I'm not the first one here," warned Leila.   Rolling up the apron and tucking it under one arm, she prepared to depart.

"That means Leila is going to walk in at the last minute with our rosebud girl on her arm," Martha Merrick declared.   "Honestly, mates, it's going to be so funny, if all works out as it should.   It will be the first definite blow we have attempted to strike.   After the way Natalie Weyman behaved on the day she volunteered to meet that Sanford crowd, she *needs* a lesson."

"What possessed her, do you suppose?" Nella Sherman asked.   "As nearly as I can remember, she insisted upon going to the train to meet them. Then she missed them, although she had plenty of time to reach the station before their train arrived. Afterward, she went to one of their rooms, I don't know which, to apologize for her non-appearance. Result, they had their dinner at Baretti's."

"What do you mean, Nella?" Martha Merrick looked nonplussed. "I don't see the connection between your last two remarks."

"I'll enlighten you. You are the one who told me that our five Sanford freshmen asked you to direct them to Baretti's that night. It was after six o'clock when they arrived at the Hall. Naturally, it took them time to scrub and generally freshen after an all day's ride on the train. What did Natalie Wyman do but decide to make them an apology call precisely at the time when they should have gone down to dinner. Miss Cairns and Dulcie Vale were with her. They stayed until after the dining room had closed. We didn't find this out, all in a minute, Martha. It took Leila, Midget, Selma and I to piece it together. You helped by remarking to us about you and Rosalind meeting them."

"Yes, and since then Natalie Weyman hardly speaks to those girls," added Selma.

"There is only one explanation for such contemptible conduct," Martha said scornfully, "and you know it as well as I. This is the first I have heard of Natalie's call. Last year she was quite friendly with me until I said to her that I thought it was ill-bred to base social values on money. She cut me after that. I was not sorry."

"She is very malicious and if she had known those five girls beforehand I would say that she had an object in playing dog in the manger about meeting them and keeping them from their dinner afterward," Leila Harper said. "As it happens, they knew no one here. They are thoroughbred to the bone. Not one word have they ever said to anyone of that night."

"It was a case of selfishness and lack of consideration, I imagine," surmised Vera Mason. "I mean, on Miss Weyman's part."

"Whatever prompted such inconsideration, I am sick of it," was Leila's vehement utterance. "Why should the fine traditions of this college be trodden under by such vandals? That's precisely what they are. We should have gone to the train to meet those girls. When it was distinctly given out that Natalie Weyman intended to go, what was our conclusion? That they belonged to her circle. I made acquaintance very warily with them, on that account. They dress as well as any of the Sans ever dreamed of dressing. Miss Warner dresses more plainly, but her gowns are pleasing. They may be the daughters of millionaires, for all we know, but they are not snobs. Have you noticed the way they have taken up nice little Miss Langly? She has actually been abused by the Sans. Why? They were determined to make her give up her room to that obnoxious little freshie, Miss Elster. I despise the ultra-sophisticated type of girl she is. She boasts that she rides to hounds, enters dachshunds at bench shows, plays billiards and so on. She swaggers about like a detestable young man instead of a young girl."

"Really, Leila, you are certainly a successful information gleaner," Nella regarded her roommate with an amused smile. "You know how to keep it to yourself, too. I hadn't heard that Miss Langly had been abused by the Sans, or, that a freshman who rode to hounds was conspiring with the Sans to snatch her room."

"You've heard now," returned Leila, the twinkle in her eye evident. "After tonight, oh, how many things we shall be hearing! After the ball is over we shall be at one, I hope, with the Sanford five. If so, then the crowd of us ought to be able to work together for a more congenial condition of affairs at the Hall. The Sans are trying hard to run it and overrun us. They make it hard for Miss Remson, and it is a shame. If enough of us stand together for our rights, they will have to respect them. They won't like us, but, then, do we admire them?"

"If things turn out tonight as we have planned, the Sans will be raving. Do you think it is perfectly fair to Miss Dean, Leila?" Vera's tones carried a slight anxiety.

"Yes, I do, Midget," came the instant reply. "She won't like it, perhaps. Still it can't do anything more than make her unpopular with the Sans. She is that, already, as I happen to know. If she is the girl I think her, she will simply pay no attention to them. Set your mind easy. We are doing her a service."

CHAPTER XVIII.

A DISCOMFITED SAN SOUCIAN.

WHEN, at eight o'clock, Leila Harper knocked on Marjorie's door, the vision who opened it brought a gleam of triumph to her bright blue eyes. Marjorie was wearing the frock of Chinese crêpe and looking her beautiful, young-girl best in it. The dress was exquisite enough in itself. Worn by her it seemed invested with fresh beauty. In turn, it lent to her a certain soft loveliness which no other frock she had ever possessed had brought out.

"Oh, my stars, what a dream you are, little Miss Dean!" praised Leila, laughingly adopting a touch of brogue which she used to perfection. Inwardly she was so delighted she could have squealed for joy. Her appraising eyes instantly picked Marjorie's frock as unique.

Veronica, who was talking animatedly to Vera, her escort, as she drew on her long gloves, looked equally charming in her own way. She was attired in an imported gown of pleated French chiffon in two shades of silvery gray. It was banded about the square neck and very short pleated sleeves with black velvet ribbon on which were embroidered a Persian pattern of silver stars. The wide black velvet ribbon sash was also thickly star-studded, as were her black satin slippers.

Jerry, who had gone on with Helen, was wearing a stunning gown of old gold satin with deeper gold embroideries. Lucy, thanks to Veronica, had had the severity of her white organdie graduation gown transformed by a fine white lace overdress which Ronny had fairly forced upon her, together with a pale green satin sash with fringed ends, a pair of embroidered white silk stockings and a pair of white satin slippers. Muriel, who had also gone ahead with her ceremonious escort, was the true Picture Girl, as Marjorie loved to call her, in a pale lavender silk net over lavender taffeta. At her belt she wore a huge bunch of lavender orchids, for which gallant Moretense had sent to New York.

The gymnasium was not far from Wayland Hall,

therefore the democratic element of sophomores who lived there had not favored taking their freshmen to the dance in automobiles. Leila Harper, Hortense Barlow and Vera Mason had their own motor cars at Hamilton, in a near-by garage, but common sense smiled at using them in preference to the short walk under the twinkling autumn stars.

"Don't forget your violets, Marjorie," called Veronica over her shoulder, as she went out the door. "I'll wait for you downstairs. Pardon me, I forgot I was being escorted," she made laughing apology to Vera. "We'll wait for you, I should have said."

"As if I could forget these darlings!" Marjorie took an immense bunch of single, long-stemmed violets from a vase of water and wiping them gently re-rolled the stems in their sheath of silver and violet paper. "They are my favorite flower," she told Leila. "They go perfectly with this frock." She pinned them securely against her sash with a quaint silver clasp pin. "There, I won't be likely to lose them!"

"Would you mind telling a poor Irish girl where under the stars that gown grew?" Leila had not been able to remove her eyes from it long at a time.

Marjorie obligingly complied, going further to

tell of the happy surprise which had attended the receipt of it.

"Your father must love you oceans," Leila said almost sadly. "My father died when I was three. I have a step-father. He is not so much to my liking. My mother and he maintain a residence in the United States, but they are in England most of the time. I live with my father's sister when I am home on vacations. She is keen on clubs and welfare work. She allows me to do as I please. What kind of life is that for a young girl?" Leila shrugged her white shoulders with true Irish melancholy. Dressed in a beautiful gown of old rose Georgette with a partial over-frock of frost-like white lace, she was a magnificent study. The combination of fine, strong features which went to make up her face, made it striking rather than beautiful.

Suddenly her brooding features broke into smiling light. "Pay no attention to me. Let's be off to the dance. Just a word before we go. I wish you would feel that I am your true friend. If, when we first met, you thought me, well—not quite frank, it was because I wished to be sure that I liked you. That's all, except, remember what I have just said about being your friend."

"I will," Marjorie promised gravely. "I shall hope always to prove myself your true friend." She offered her hand.

Leila took it and shook it vigorously. "Now we have a bargain," she said. "Never forget it."

In the lower hall they found Ronny and Vera Mason waiting, and the four stopped only long enough to cover their fine raiment, temporarily, with evening capes. During the short walk through the soft fall night Leila made them all laugh with her funny sallies. She had apparently lost her recent pensive mood. Nevertheless at intervals that evening the hopeless melancholy of her tone came back to Marjorie. She thought Leila must have been born in Ireland, for she was at times utterly un-American in her manner of speaking.

The scene of festivity upon which they presently came was one of color and light. The great room was already well-filled with merry-makers, each in her prettiest gown. From a corner of the room, screened by palms and huge branches of red and yellow autumn leaves, an orchestra was playing a *valse lente*. That the sophs had outdone anything for several years in the way of artistic decorations was the opinion of the faculty, present almost to a member. Though they graciously lent their presence to an affair, such as the freshmen's frolic, they obligingly left the dance early, rarely remaining more than an hour.

The San Soucians were well represented in the receiving line, the majority having been appointed to it by their ally, Joan Myers. Lined up, they made a gorgeous appearance. The majority of them were attired in frocks of striking colors and displayed considerable jewelry. Looking up and down the long row, it seemed to Marjorie that she glimpsed the white fire of diamonds on every girl that composed it. It struck her as rather ridiculous that, so long as the Sans Soucians snubbed the majority of the students, they should wish to be on a committee to receive the very girls they affected not to know.

"Be easy," remarked Leila, in a tone which only Ronny, Vera and Marjorie heard. "We are to run the one-sided gauntlet, it seems. Let us be about it and have it done. Follow your leader and not too much cordiality. They have none for us, though they will be sweet on the surface."

These being the first remarks of the kind Marjorie had heard Leila make, she glanced at the latter rather searchingly. Leila was not looking at her. Her eyes were playing up and down the receiving line, a world of veiled contempt in their blue depths.

As the quartette approached the row of brightly-garbed young women, Joan Myers, who stood at its head, bent a steady stare upon Marjorie. Next she turned to the girl on her left and muttered in her ear. The latter chanced to be Natalie Weyman, resplendent in an apricot satin frock, with over panels of seed pearls on satin and a garniture of the same at the very low bodice. The gown was sleeveless, and smacked more of the stage than of a college frolic. A cluster of peculiar orange and white orchids trailed across one shoulder. These Marjorie could honestly admire. Of Natalie's gown she did not approve.

At sight of Marjorie, Natalie's face grew dark. Nor did the further sight of Veronica improve her sulky expression. How she managed to smile and murmur a few words of welcome she hardly knew. She was literally seething with jealous rage at the two freshmen. Her eyes did not deceive her as to the distinction of their frocks. She knew after a first appraising glance that there were no others in the room to compete with them. They were the unobtainable so far as money went. They were the kind of frocks that only proper influence might secure. She forgot her earlier grudge against Marjorie's loveliness in jealousy viewing her later offense.

Piloted by Leila, the quartette made short work of being received by as chilly a lot of young patronesses as jealousy could furnish. When they had won clear of the receiving line, Leila indulged in a subdued ripple of laughter.

"Oh, my heart, but were they not icy?" she inquired, her eyes dancing. "Vera, did you see Nat Weyman's face? She used to be jealous of you. Now she has other trouble to worst."

"Don't mind Leila's outbreak," Vera turned to Marjorie and Ronny who were looking eagerly about them, charmed by the animated scene. "She can't endure Natalie Weyman, and neither can I. This is not the place to say such things, but we are not fond of the Sans and we had rather you knew it. It will help you to understand much that may happen later on." Vera colored as she said this. She felt that it would in a measure mitigate any displeasure that Marjorie in particular might afterward feel for Leila.

"We do not know much of the Sans Soucians, but we are not in favor of snobs," Ronny made steady utterance. She had seen the dark glance Natalie Weyman had leveled at Marjorie, and quite understood Leila's comments. She could also understand why Vera had aroused the vain sophomore's jealousy. Vera's white chiffon frock over pale green taffeta, made her look like a fairy queen who might have stepped from the heart of a wihte flower to attend the frolic.

"We know that. Otherwise you might be escorting yourselves here for all Vera and I should care," returned Leila with a genial smile that was irresistible. "Let us bury them deep, as we say in

Kilarney, and have a good time. I wish you to meet two or three pets of mine among the seniors. Then off to the dance we shall wend. I tell you now, I am a fine Irish gentleman when it comes to playing the part at a hop."

With Leila doing the honors, the two Lookouts had a lively time for the next half hour. Though the dancing had begun, she insisted upon parading the three girls from one end of the gymnasium to the other. She appeared to have a wide acquaintance among the juniors and the seniors. Consequently Ronny and Marjorie met girls they had seen on the campus, but whom as upper class young women they had hardly hoped to meet.

When they finally joined in the dancing, which both had been longing to do, they were soon besieged with invitations. It was such a complete surprise to both, which they refused mentally to stop and think about it, preferring to drift comfortably along on the tide of youthful enjoyment. It was an hour after their arrival before they had an opportunity to talk with Jerry, Lucy and Muriel. All three had been enjoying themselves hugely. Lucy had had an interesting, though short, talk with Professor Wenderblatt, the director of the biology department, whose daughter, Lillian, was a freshman. She had met them both through Katherine. The latter and herself were now rejoicing in an invitation to dinner at the Wenderblatts on the following Sunday.

Jerry, according to her own enthusiastic version, was simply falling all over herself with happiness. Helen was the "Prince of Hamilton" when it came to playing escort. Muriel was no less pleased. She gigglingly confided to her chums that Moretense was considerably less tense when she danced than she had expected to find her.

The delightful evening had winged its way toward eleven o'clock when, after a spirited fox trot, the bell in the gymnasium clanged out the five strokes which stood for "attention" at Hamilton. Instant with the last stroke, a breathless silence fell. It was broken by a high-pitched call from one side of the gymnasium. From an ante room a figure in a page's costume of hunter's green darted out and ran to the center of the floor. Trumpet to her lips, the sophomore page played a lively little rondelay. It was answered from the ante room on the opposide and another page, similarly clad, joined the first. Another fanfare of trumpets and three figures in dark brown robes with immense snow-white wigs appeared from the left-hand ante-room.

"Hear ye! Hear ye! Comes now a friende to Beautye brighte. An ye are fair, O, maid, the Beautye crowne shall win ye! Mayhap, mayhap! An ye are fair!"

The voice of the central be-wigged figure echoed through the room. The owner was a senior who sang bass in the Idlehour Glee Club, hence the robust tones.

"What is it to be? I don't understand," was whispered about the room.

CHAPTER XIX.

THE GIFTE OF BEAUTYE.

"OH, I know what this is going to be," Helen Trent informed Jerry under her breath. "It's an old Celtic beauty contest. Away back in the history of the Celts, they set aside one day in the year for games and contests. Just at sunset came the beauty contest. The Brown Judges, there are always three, who were in charge of all ethical matters. for the Celts had their own ideas about ethics, came down from their writing in the court tower and made this proclamation. All the pretty girls and women in the village would enter it. The judges would take their places on the fiddler's platform and the beauty line had to pass them three times in slow succession. As they knew everyone in their village, I suppose it wasn't very hard for them to pick the winner! She was accorded thereupon," Helen quoted from memory, " 'the acclamation of her people, and, added to the joy of knowledge of Beauty, a silver purse, containing three heavy gold pieces, together with a solemn adjuration to do well, breed no vanity of the mind and say a prayer of thankfulness at even for the gift of Beauty, by the grace of God.' "

"How pretty," Jerry said softly. "Well, if this is a beauty contest, I hope the judges won't be partial. I know whom I think ought to win it."

"You mean Marjorie?" Helen asked guardedly. "I think so too. Now listen to this charge to the contestants. I know it pretty well. Leila Harper let me take a book on the Celts. She brought it with her from Ireland. She was born in Dublin and came to this country when she was twelve. She is at the bottom of this and I know why. The clever maneuverer that she is!" Helen laughed, then her face suddenly sobered. She glanced anxiously at Marjorie, who stood not far away, her brown eyes riveted on the three judges. The conditions of the contest were about to be laid down by one of them.

"One makes this charge to winsome maids, not all may win the crowne! All ye who are to Beautye bent have had the assurance long. No mirrore 'flects a fairness back there be no fairenesse there.

The twisted eye, the fanged tooth, the loose-lippede mouth, the mottlede skin, the unclassike nose, the sharpenede chin are not of Beautye's kin. Beare this in mind and venture not 'fore the Judges' critike heighte an ye are cursede with these. Now not too talle, nor yet too lowe; e're be ye passinge faire. The heighte of man, five feete and nine, is not our favore gainede. Nor is the midge of four feete teyne, more than the olde, olde childe. Of grace we thinke on heavilye and note the free lighte step, the slendyre carriage of the budding flower, whiche she of grace does have. Of frank sweete looke, yet not so bolde, we rank as beautied worth. No countenance is perfecte yet when guile lurkes backe its eyese. So shalle ye rate yourselvese in mind upon our honeste scale, spokyne in hones klaryte to save the injuryede feeling of the sex, and we who judge ye much of vexede delaye and crude annoye. Beare last of all this sacrede truthe, goode Beautye needs no artifyce. The cosmetykes of cheatynge maides are instante knowne to use to be abhorrede."

With this pointed laying down of entrance conditions to the contest, His Honor, the center judge, and the tallest of the three, fell back a little, to allow his companion on the left to speak. With a dramatic wave of the arms he began:

"Upon yon heighte we now shalle stand to sighte ye as ye passe." A second sweep of the arm designated a small platform profusely decorated in hunter's green, the freshman class color. and old gold, that of the sophomore class. It stood near the big Japanese lemonade bowl and had excited considerable curiosity during the evening, as no one seemed to know its purpose.

The third judge, who had thus far been silent, now called out in a veritable town-crier voice: "Heede ye! Heede ye! Beautye waites her worthynge. Lyne ye single fylinge. Passe ye once before us! Passe ye twice before us! Passe ye thryce before us! Walke ye to slowe measure."

Having delivered himself of these succinct directions, the speaker joined his companions in bowing low to the enthralled assemblage. Whereupon, all three turned and strode majestically toward the fateful platform. Luckily the builders of the stand had not forgotten to place two makeshift steps of soap boxes, carpeted in green. The august judges had also been cautioned beforehand to tread upon them lightly or run a chance of disgracing their high and mighty personages by an ignominious tumble.

While they were disposing themselves on the platform with as much dignity as a wary ascent would allow, their hearers were fascinatedly considering the proclamation. Hardly a young girl who does not take a pardonable interest in a beauty contest. While she may be honestly sure that she would never be chosen the winner, she has a secret desire to enter it simply because she is a young girl.

From all parts of the gymnasium a subdued murmur of voices now arose, mingled with much soft laughter. Thus far the proclamation was too new to court action. Besides, it took temerity, after hearing the conditions, to walk boldly forth, an aspirant for beauty honors. Finally a knot of juniors, who had been loitering near the Judges' stand exchanging pleasantries with the brown-robed critics, obeyed a mischievous impulse to start the ball rolling. Forming into line, these six, none of whom had a claim to more than fairly good looks, marched solemnly out onto the floor and approached the stand at an exaggeratedly slow walk. A shout of mirth arose, which they acknowledged with wide smiles. The ice was broken, however, and the line began to grow amazingly. At each end of the room, the two pages had now taken up their station in order to direct the progress of the beauty line.

"Catch me joining that line," declared Jerry. "I know just how beautiful I am without any opinions from those three old wigs."

"You goose!" exclaimed Helen, in an undertone. "Come on. There's Muriel just going into line with Miss Barlow." She giggled at the idea of stiff Moretense courting beauty honors. "If Marjorie sees all of us in it she will join, too. Otherwise she will stay out of it, and Veronica along with her. Either one of them are positively stunning types. Only I would vote for Marjorie. She really is the prettiest girl I ever saw. Why, on the campus now, the really worth-while girls rave over her."

"Maybe the judges won't see it that way, deprecated Jerry. "Do you know them?"

"Yes, I do. They are all right. Leila picked them and she is always fair. I told you this was her work. Now come on." Helen slipped an arm into Jerry's and towed her, unresisting, into the long line that was now moving decorously around the gymnasium. Needless to say, the Sans had joined it. Even Lola Elster, accompanied by Leslie Cairns, had swaggered into line. Both had arrived late, attired in expensive, but somewhat flashy fall sports suits and hats. Neither removed her hat when dancing, a proceeding which many of the juniors and seniors present regarded with no leniency. The Sans appeared to consider this rude ignoring of convention a huge joke. Lola Elster's impudent face bespoke her satisfaction in having thus defied the canons of good taste.

By the time the entire procession had passed the judges' stand once, fully two-thirds of the company had joined it. Marjorie had been among the last to do so. Even then she would have preferred to stay out of the contest, had not Leila insisted that she must take part in it, pointing out to her Jerry, Muriel, and greatly to her surprise, Ronny, among the aspirants.

"It is only for fun, modest child," argued Leila, in her most persuasive tones. She had foreseen this very snag in the way of her plan. Already the line had passed the stand for the second time. "Ah, come on!" she implored, catching Marjorie by the hand.

With a half sigh of reluctance, Marjorie yielded. Next second, Leila was hurrying her across the lower end of the room where the last of the procession was just rounding a corner. At least a third of the guests had elected to stay out of the contest. From different points of the gymnasium arose an energetic clapping of hands as Marjorie and Leila caught up with the line. Leila chuckled under her breath. Marjorie's reluctance had only served to strengthen her chances for winning. Leila knew that the judges' decision could not be attacked. She had been careful to select three seniors whose word was law at Hamilton. If they pronounced Marjorie Dean the most beautiful girl present, then, undoubtedly, she was.

As for Marjorie, she felt her face flame until it seemed to her that it must be bright vermilion.

She experienced a momentary desire to upbraid Leila for thus bringing her into such undesired notice. She had not realized how conspicuous their cutting across the corner had made them until the applause had begun. Walking ahead of Leila, she was so chagrined at her own stupidity that she moved along mechanically, hardly cognizant of what was happening.

It seemed a long time to her before the line completed its third tour of the room. Came an echoing order from one of the judges to halt and the contestants obeyed with admirable alacrity. Part of them were viewing the beauty judges with smiles, perfectly content in knowing they would not be chosen. To a number, however, the contest had taken on a serious aspect. Two very pretty freshmen, pets of the Sans, stood looking at the judges as though determined to force their approval. Among the Sans Soucians there was an element of alertness that pointed to a smug belief in their claim to beauty.

Of the contestant, none was more concerned in the decision than Natalie Weyman. For a whole college year she had been acclaimed as the Hamilton College beauty. While considerable of this reputation had been built up for her by the Sans, it had gained ground, for one reason or another. She had taken care to live up to it, spending time and

money in the cause of her personal adornment.
Now, after having fought hard for it, she did not
propose to relinquish it. She was inwardly furious
over the contest. There were half a dozen girls
whom she feared, all looking radiantly lovely.
Vera Mason had never looked prettier. Martha
Merrick was simply stunning in that maize tissue
gown. More than once that evening Natalie had
watched Muriel with a frown. But those other two
hateful girls! Her envy had been thoroughly
aroused by Marjorie's and Ronny's gowns. Her
jealousy was rampant because of the beauty of their
wearers. Though nothing could have forced from
her the truth, she knew that the palm belonged to
Marjorie.

Standing a little in front of a group of her
friends, where she might be plainly seen by the
judges, she assumed an attitude in which a portrait
painter had posed her for a portrait the previous
winter. Having slyly loosened one of the orchids
from the cluster she was wearing, she began pick-
ing it to pieces, her head slightly bent. Falling
into the pose with consummate art of the practiced
deceiver, she really made an attractive study.

Marjorie and Leila had halted almost the length
of the gymnasium from Natalie, to Leila's inward
vexation. She had hoped to see the two brought
close together. She was sternly determined to see

the false colors stripped from Natalie Weyman, whom she despised for a just reason which no one but herself knew.

"Let us have faith that the judges have good eyesight," she muttered, as the judge who had delivered the charge to "Beautye brighte" held up a brown-winged arm for silence.

If the single gesture had been a wizard's charm, it could hardly have taken effect more quickly. A hush, almost painful, ensued. The roll of the spokesman's announcing tones fairly jarred the absolute stillness.

"Upon our queste of Beautye brighte, we have not soughte in vaine. So manye maides of faire young pryde make hard the chosynge then. Nor had the taske been done e'en yet, walkyede Beautye not amongst ye. On Mystresse Marjorie, of the Deans, our critike favor falles. Beautye has she to bless the eye and satisfye the heart."

A murmur of acclamation began with the announcement of Marjorie's name. It increased in volume until it drowned the judge's speech. "Delighted," that dignitary managed to shout so as to be heard, and, with a profound bow, waited for the noise to subside.

Standing beside Leila, who was applauding vigorously, a positive Cheshire-cat grin on her usually indifferent face, Marjorie fervently wished that she might suddenly drop through the floor. Her em-. barrassment was so great that she hardly knew in which direction to look or what to do. When quiet again descended the judge went on with the rest of a very complimentary speech. It ended in a summons to come to the stand and be acclaimed Beautye and receive Beautye's guerdon.

At this Marjorie absolutely balked. Neither could Leila nor several other students, who had gathered round her, persuade her to go forward. It ended by a flushed and half indignant Beautye being forcibly marched up to the stand by a crowd of laughing girls. The guerdon was an immense bunch of long-stemmed American Beauty roses. Marjorie made a never-to-be-forgotten picture, as surrounded by her body guard, she stood with her arms full of roses and listened to the quaint adjuration to Beautye.

Unbidden tears crowded to her eyes as the judge ended with fine dramatic expression: "Brede ye, therefore sweete maids, no vanitye of the mind, but, say ye raythere, at even, a prayer of thankfulnesse for the gifte of Beautye, by the grace of God." The emotional side of her nature touched by the fineness of the sentiment, she forgot herself as its object.

A group of Silverton Hall girls, headed by Portia Graham and Robin Page, gathered to offer their warm congratulations. Entirely against her will, Marjorie Dean, Hamilton College freshman, had been accorded an honor which she had neither expected nor desired.

CHAPTER XX.

LIVING UP TO TRADITION.

To be ignored on one's arrival at Hamilton and in less than six weeks to be acclaimed the college beauty seemed the very irony of fate to Marjorie. The week following the freshman frolic was a hard one for her. Used to going unostentatiously about with her chums, she now found herself continually in the limelight. Whenever she appeared on the campus she had the uncomfortable feeling that every movement of hers was being watched.

"You may thank your stars that you are at college where the newspapers aren't allowed to trespass," Ronny had laughingly assured her when she complained. Nevertheless she was far from pleased when a prominent illustrator wrote her a polite note asking permission to make sketches of her. Worse still, she received later a letter from a New York theatrical manager offering her an engagement in a musical comedy he was about to launch. How either man had come into knowledge of her name she could not imagine.

While she had been deeply annoyed at the artist's note, she grew angry at the temerity of the theatrical manager and promptly tore the letter into shreds. How she wished that she had never allowed herself to be dragged into that foolish beauty contest. Afterward Leila had candidly owned to Marjorie her part in the affair. While Marjorie had been obliged to laugh at the Irish girl's clever move against the Sans, she had wondered whether she really liked Leila. Instead of being pleased over her triumph, she was distinctly put out about it.

"I never saw you so near to being really downright cross as you've been since that old beauty contest," observed Jerry one afternoon in late October, as Marjorie entered the room, a frown between her brows, a tired droop to her pretty mouth.

"I *feel* like being downright cross," emphasized Marjorie, accompanying the last three words with three energetic slams of her book on chemistry on the table. "I wish this popularity business were in Kamchatka. I thought I would like to take a walk around the campus today, all by myself, and think about what I would write this evening. I have to write a theme for poetics to be handed in tomorrow morning. I wasn't allowed a minute to myself. There are some awfully nice girls here, but I wasn't anxious for company today. I haven't the least idea what I shall write and I wanted to save time by choosing my subject this afternoon."

"Go and ask Ronny for a subject," calmly advised Jerry. "She loves poems, poets and poetics in general. She is in her room writing to her father. She fired me out, but you may have better luck. She may have fiuished writing. It seems a long while since she inhospitably requested me to make myself scarce. My, but you are sympathetic!" Marjorie was already half way through the door, regardless of Jerry's plaint.

"Come in," called Ronny, in response to Marjorie's two measured raps. "Oh, Marjorie, I was just coming to see you. I have a piece of news for you."

"Come along," invited Marjorie, "but first give me a subject for a theme for poetics. "I need one in a hurry. Jerry said you were authority on the subject."

"I am amazed at her charity," chuckled Ronny, "after the way I shooed her away from my door."

"She mentioned it," returned Marjorie significantly, whereupon both girls laughed.

"Let me see," pondered Ronny. "Why don't you write on the genius Poe as above that of any other American poet? Illustrate by quoting from other poets and then comparing the excerpts with his work. Read his essay on poetry tonight before you begin to write. It will give you inspiration. I brought a five volume set of Poe from home. Here's the volume containing the essay you need."

Ronny took from a near-by book-case the desired volume and handed it to Marjorie.

"Thank you." Marjorie accepted it gratefully. "I believe I *can* write a fairly good theme on that subject. I have always admired Poe's work."

"I adore his memory," asserted Veronica solemnly. "I have read every scrap I could find concerning him. He ranked next to Shakespeare in genius. I know he was an earnest worker and a good man. I am sure that he was not a drunkard, but a terribly maligned genius. He was purposely kept down through jealousy and had to sell the products of his genius for a copper. He suffered terribly, but I imagine he had the inner happiness of knowing that not one brilliant emanation of his master mind could be snatched from him by the unworthy."

Veronica's gray eyes flashed in sympathy for the misunderstood man whose transcendental genius made him an outlander among the writers of his period.

"Again I thank you. This time for your lecture." Marjorie bobbed up and down twice in quick succession. "I'll try to put some of it into my theme. Now for my room, and the news."

Jerry pretended not to see Ronny until she was well inside the room. She then rose up, and, in a purposely gruff voice, ordered her out. Needless to say, Ronny was not to be intimidated.

"No, Jeremiah, I shall not budge an inch. Here you sit doing nothing. Why shouldn't I come in and sit on Marjorie's side of the room? I have news to impart—n-e-w-s," spelled Ronny.

At this Jerry pricked up her ears and became suddenly affable.

"I heard today," began Ronny impressively, "that there will be a basket ball try-out next Friday afternoon in the gym, at four-thirty."

"That's cheering news!" Marjorie's sober features lightened. "Where did you hear it, Ronny?"

"Miss Page told me. The notices will appear in a day or two. She played on a team all the time she was at Wildreth, a prep school she was graduated from. Naturally she is anxious to make the team this year."

"I'd like to play," Marjorie said wistfully. "I suppose I won't stand much chance among so many, though."

"Well, you won the Beauty contest," cited Jerry wickedly. "That was a case of one in a multitude."

Marjorie rose and going over to where Jerry sat,

waved her book menacingly over her room-mate's
head. "Dare to say another word about that hateful old contest and I'll disown you," she threatened.
"I want to forget all about it, if I can. Basket ball
is different, thank goodness. If I make the freshman team, I have actually achieved something."

"I hope you make it." Jerry spoke with a sudden sincerity arising from her devotion to Marjorie.
"Muriel will try for it. Moretense is too tense to
make a startling player. Shall you try for it,
Ronny?"

"No, indeed," Ronny answered. You and Lucy
and I will be fans. I am not very partial to basket
ball unless the game happens to move fast. Then
I grow interested. Miss Page says the seniors are
managing the sports. They usually do. A senior
told her of the try-out."

"Did Miss Page say anything else about it?"
quizzed Jerry.

"No; she heard only that. She said she thought
the sports committee were purposely keeping back
the information. The senior who told her overheard the two of the committee talking to Miss
Reid, the physical instructor. She happened to be
in the gymnasium at the time. She was not asked
to keep it secret, so she felt at liberty to mention it
to me."

Jerry regarded Ronny in silence for a moment.

"This college makes me weary," she burst out in an impatient voice. "There are too many undercurrents here. Why should the sports committee keep back information about basket ball? To suit their own pleasure, of course. Very likely they are banded into a clique like those silly Sans Soucians. If it happens to be the same kind of clique, then look out for trouble at the try-out."

"Perhaps they have a good reason for not giving out the information until a certain time," argued Ronny. "Maybe they don't approve of the Sans. As seniors, they should be on the heights, so far as college ethics are concerned."

"I trust they are," Jerry returned, in a prim voice, rolling her eyes at Ronny. "Just the same, I doubt it. I'll tell you more about 'em after the try-out. They'll have to show me."

It was on Monday that Ronny heard of the try-out. Not until Thursday afternoon did the notices of it appear on the various bulletin boards. Their advent led to a certain amount of jubilation on the part of those freshmen who were fond of the game. When, at four-thirty, the next afternoon, the committee appeared in company with Miss Reid, they found at least thirty-five of the freshman class as aspirants to the team. A part of the unaspiring members had come to look on. There was also a large percentage of sophomores on the scene. Outside the committee there was only a sprinkling of juniors and seniors.

Marjorie and Muriel had put on their gymnasium suits at the Hall and had arrived at the gymnasium shortly after four o'clock. Jerry, Ronny and Lucy did not appear until almost half-past four. They were accompanied by Vera Mason, Nella Sherman and Leila Harper. In the meantime Marjorie and Muriel had been watching, with some longing, a number of freshmen who were out on the floor practicing with the ball. Prominent among them was Lola Elster, who seemed to know the game, or thought she did, better than her companion player. She was quite in her element, and was issuing frequent orders, in a rather shrill voice, as she darted about in pursuit of the ball. The "pick-up" squad with whom she was playing appeared to be completely under her domination.

"I don't care to make a team that Miss Elster is on," Muriel confided to Marjorie in a disgusted tone. "She is altogether too fond of her own playing. Besides, she is inclined to be tricky and I wouldn't trust her. She'd elbow her best friend out of the way if they were both after the ball."

"Those girls seem to like her," commented Marjorie. "I should say none of them were very good players. It is conceited, perhaps, to say that we know the game better than they, but if that is a sample of their work, we are stars compared with them. They couldn't make more than a scrub team at Sanford High."

"I know it," agreed Muriel. "They aren't quick enough. That's their greatest trouble." Glancing from the players to the audience, who stood in groups about the room, she exclaimed: "There are the girls! Let's go over and see them."

"Only for a minute," Marjorie stipulated. "This affair is going to begin soon."

They had no more than exchanged a few words with their chums when the bell rang for a clear floor. Incidental with it the senior manager of basket ball interests stepped forward to make the usual announcements for the try-out and lay down the conditions which the players must observe. Those wishing to try for a place on the regular freshman team were then requested to come forward on the floor. About thirty-five girls responded and enough of them to make two squads were selected. These were ordered to the floor for a twenty-minutes' test. Their work was carefully noted by Miss Reid, three seniors, including the manager, and a Mr. Fulton, a professional coach.

Altogether, four sets of players were tried out. Several of the freshmen who had worked on the first squads did duty again. Among these was

Lola Elster. It was among the third round of players that Marjorie and Muriel appeared, and only half-heartedly at that. Both felt the utter futility of trying for the team, after they had looked on for a little. They did not like the methods of either the coach or Miss Reid. Neither were expert in proper knowledge of the game. Worse, their sympathies were plainly with Miss Elster, who, when not on the floor, stood between them, talking animatedly, now indicating one or another of the players, or expressing an opinion to which both agreed by nodding affably.

Both Lookouts made a conscientious effort to play their best, but their team mates were fit only for scrub players. The result was the slowest twenty minutes' work that either ever remembered. Try as they might, they could not overcome the disadvantage under which they were laboring. Hardest of all was the knowledge that they could make a good showing if they but had the opportunity.

When their time was up both gladly hurried from the floor to where their group of friends awaited them. The expressions of the five girls varied only in the degree of contempt each registered for what they had just witnessed.

"Why didn't you wait to see whether you made the team?" inquired Jerry with gentle sarcasm.

"A-h-h-h!" was Muriel's reply, expressive of her feelings.

"We couldn't make that team in a century." Marjorie was smiling a whimsical little smile which contained no bitterness.

"I guess not. You might as well have played for twenty minutes with a bunch of nine-pins. Anyway, you were dead before you ever set foot on the floor. That Miss Elster has the coach, Miss Reid and several others right on her side. This is the Sans inning, n'est ce pas? Uh-huh! No mistake about it." Jerry bowed and smirked as she carried on this bit of conversation with herself.

"Cast an eye upon the Sans just now," Leila said scornfully. "Are they not pleased with themselves? Do you think they would have let you or Muriel make that team? Not so long as they could influence those in charge. The seniors are not to blame. They kept the date of the try-out to themselves until the last to prevent the Sans from fixing things for their freshman friends. It did small good." Leila shrugged her shoulders.

"They shouldn't be allowed to run things," Jerry asserted stoutly. The trouble is everyone stands back and allows them to take the lead. Their cast-iron nerve is what helps them out. Besides they are an unscrupulous lot. They boast that they are the daughters of millionaires. Well, the rest of us are not paupers. Only we are above trading upon our folks' money as a means of influence. That is ignoble and should be stamped out of Hamilton."

"It never will be unless we all work together for a new spirit of democracy," broke in Ronny's resolute tones. "We must establish it in our class regardless of these unfair sophomores and their false notions, so detrimental to nobility of character."

"Unfair indeed." Leila smiled wryly. "Vera and I know. You should have seen us last year. We had a disagreeable freshman cruise, thanks to the Sans. They thought for a short time that we were perhaps poor. We found it out and let them think so to their hearts' content. You should have seen their scorn of us. At Thanksgiving we had our cars sent on to us. Then they were in a quandary! We were not poor, so it seemed, but how wealthy were we? They never found out. They tried so hard."

A blast of the manager's whistle signalled attention. The names of the successful contestans were about to be read out by the coach. Lola Elster had been awarded center. Two of her particular friends had won right and left guard. Robina Page had achieved right forward. At this, none watching wondered. She had played in the first squads and done good work. Left forward fell to a Miss Burton, a freshman Dulcie Vale had been rushing and whom she had escorted to the frolic.

"I am glad it is over. I am not sorry I tried for a place on the team," soliloquized Marjorie aloud. "Neither Muriel nor I had a fair chance. I was hurt and disappointed for a minute or so after I saw the way things were going. I am not now. I shall wait until next year," she announced, in a calm, determined voice, "then I shall make the team. That means we will all have to work to-gether to bring about a happier state of affairs at Hamilton. None of us can be free or happy with this shadow hanging over us. There can be no true class spirit unless we base it on the traditions which Mr. Brooke Hamilton wished observed by the students of Hamilton College."

CHAPTER XXI.

ON THE EVE OF THE GAME.

FOLLOWING the basket ball try-out, which the Sanford five agreed was the tamest attempt at play-ing basket ball that they had ever witnessed, little of moment befell them as the days slipped by and the Thanksgiving holiday drew near. As they would have four days' vacation, all were determined on spending them in Sanford. Ronny was going to Miss Archer's, as she had promised her God-mother this holiday before leaving for college.

Lucy Warner was the only one of the Five Travelers who intended to remain at Hamilton during the holiday. She had flatly refused to allow Ronny to defray her expense home.

"There is no use in my going home. I would not see Mother except for a very short time. She is nursing a fever patient and won't be able to leave her for at least three weeks. Yes, I know I could be with you girls. I'd love to, but Katherine has no place to go. I might better stay here with her. I am going home for Christmas and she has promised to spend those holidays with me." This was Lucy's view of the matter.

The day of their departure for home was typical Thanksgiving weather, fairly cold, and marked by snow flurries. If the trip to Hamilton had seemed long, the journey home was longer. With all four impatiently counting the miles between Hamilton and Sanford, time dragged. Their train having left Hamilton at eleven o'clock that morning, it was after dark when it pulled into Sanford. A fond company of home folks were on the station platform to greet the travelers, who for the first time since leaving for college, separated, to go in different directions.

Marjorie thought the most beautiful sight she had ever looked upon were the lights of her own dear home. Encircled by her captain's arm, they blinked her a mellow, cheery welcome as the automobile sped up the drive. She never forgot the wondrous happiness she experienced in returning to her father and mother after her first long absence from them.

It was after dark on the Sunday evening following Thanksgiving when four of the Five Travelers alighted from the train at Hamilton station. Tired though she was, and a little sad, Marjorie thrilled with an odd kind of patriotism as the lights of the campus houses twinkled on her horizon. There was, after all, a certain vague joy in having returned to college.

Ronny, Jerry and Muriel all agreed with her in this, as the Lookouts gathered in hers and Jerry's room after Sunday night supper to tell Lucy the news of home. Mrs. Warner had called at the Deans on Saturday and intrusted a letter and package to Marjorie for Lucy. The package, when opened, revealed a pretty knitted sweater and cap in a warm shade of blue. Lucy's mother had knitted them during intervals while her patient slept.

"How have things been here?" queried Jerry, after the admiring comments relative to Lucy's cap and sweater had subsided.

"It has been so blissfully quiet," sighed Lucy. "There were only five girls here over Thanksgiving. Miss Remson says she has experienced a spell of heavenly calm. We had a fine Thanksgiving dinner. Two of Miss Remson's nephews were here for the day. They brought their violins and Miss Remson plays well on the piano. We had music Thanksgiving evening. Friday evening we were both invited to Professor Wenderblatt's home. Mr. Henry Arthur Bradburn, a friend of his, who has made a number of Arctic journeys is visiting him. There were about twenty-five guests. You can imagine how proud Kathie and I were. Lillian came over on Friday morning and invited us."

"You may go to the head of the class," commented Jerry. "Your're graduated from the stay-in-your-shell period. I never before heard of such a sudden and unparalleled blossoming into the high-brows' garden."

The Five Travelers lingered to talk that evening until the last minute before the ten-thirty bell rang. The next day was not characterized by particularly brilliant recitations on the part of any of the returned students.

On the third day of December notices appeared on the bulletin board announcing the first basket ball game of the season. The sophomores had challenged the freshmen to meet them on the second

Saturday in the month, which fell on the fourteenth. The sophomore team was composed entirely of Sans Soucians. Natalie Weyman, Dulcie Vale, Joan Myers, Adelaide Forman and Evangeline Heppler were the select five who were to wrestle with the freshmen for the ball.

"Can they play basket ball?" was Muriel Harding's pertinent question put to her room-mate, Miss Barlow, who had just finished naming the players on the sophomore team. The two girls had met outside Hamilton Hall and stopped as was their wont to consult the main bulletin board.

"They are fairly fast players, but," Miss Barlow's eye-brows went up, "they are so tricky. They composed the freshman team, last year. Gratifying, isn't it, to be able to head basket ball two years in succession?" The question was freighted with sarcasm.

"Very," returned Muriel, inwardly amazed at this new attitude on the part of her reserved roommate. It was the first time Moretense had ever grown personal in regard to any of the students.

"I am positive the juniors won't play them this year," Hortense continued. They had enough of them last. Really, the umpire nearly wore herself out shrieking 'foul' during that game. My word, but they worked hard—cheating. It did them not a particle of good. They lost by ten points."

"Do you like basket ball?" Muriel was further astonished at her companion's apparent interest in the sport.

"Yes, I do, when it is well and fairly played. I have never yet seen a really clever game played at Hamilton."

Similar information drifted to the Lookouts concerning the sophomores' work at basket ball, during the few days that preceded the game. Far from the usual amount of enthusiasm which attends this sport was exhibited by the upper class students. The freshmen, however, were duly excited over it. While many of them had disapproved the partiality shown at the try-out, they could only hope that the freshman team would rally to their work on the day of the game and vanquish the sophs. The team was practicing assiduously. That was a good sign. The sophomores were not nearly so faithful at practice.

"If 'our crowd' can play even half as well as the scrub teams could at Sanford High they can whip this aggregation of geese, Robin Page excepted," Jerry asserted scornfully to her chums on the evening before the game. The next day's recitations hastily prepared, the Lookouts had gathered in Ronny's room for a spread.

"I feel sorry for Miss Page," remarked Ronny, without lifting her eyes from their watch on the chafing dish in which the chocolate had begun to bubble.

"So do I. I told her so yesterday," confessed Muriel. "I met her in the library and we had quite a long talk. She said she would have resigned after the first day of practice, but she felt that it would be cowardly. She knows the game as it should be played, but the other four girls are quite shaky on some points of it and they won't let her correct them when they make really glaring mistakes. She tried it twice. Both times she just escaped quarrelling with them. So she quit."

"I think she is so plucky to stay on the team under such circumstances." Marjorie looked up from her sandwich-making labors, her face full of honest admiration for Robin. "She is such a delightful girl, isn't she?"

"She makes me think of a small boy," was Jerry's comparison. "Tell you something else about her when I get this tiresome bottle of olives opened. If I don't extract the treacherous old cork very gently, I'm due to hand myself a quarter of a bottle of brine in the eyes or in my lap or wherever it may happen to land. There!" She triumphantly drew forth the stubborn cork without accident. "Now about Robin Page. She asked me to ask you girls to go to the game with the Silverton Hall crowd. Then she wants us to be her guests at dinner at the Hall and spend the evening with her and her pals. I've accepted for us all, so make your plans accordingly."

"I've already asked Moretense to go to the game with us." Muriel looked briefly perplexed. "I don't think anyone will care if I ask her to go with us to meet the Silverton Hall girls. I can't go with you folks to dinner, for my estimable room-mate has invited me to the Colonial and engaged a table ahead. I am to meet Miss Angier and Miss Thompson, juniors and friends of hers."

"When did you make all these dates and right over our heads?" Jerry quizzed, trying to appear offended and failing utterly.

"Oh, the other day," returned Muriel lightly. "It shows you that I am well thought of, too, in high-brow circles." She cast a sly glance toward Lucy. The latter was happily engaged in cutting generous slices from a fruit cake which had come by express that day. Mrs. Warner had made it early in the fall and had put it away to season. It had arrived at an opportune time, and Lucy had gladly contributed to the feast.

She chuckled softly over Muriel's good-natured thrust, but made no reply. It was her chief pleasure to listen to her chums, rather than talk. While she had expanded wonderfully as a result of association with a fun-loving, talkative quartette of girls who had taken pains to draw her out, she still had spells of the old reserve. She was gradually growing used to the gay badinage, which went on constantly among her chums, and on rare occasions would convulse them by some dry remark of her own.

While the Five Travelers were preparing their little feast in the utmost good fellowship, in a room two doors farther up the hall five other girls sat around a festal table, arguing in an anything but equable manner. Four of them were members of the sophomore team. The fifth was Leslie Cairns.

"It's not fair to the kid if you girls don't give her a chance to win." Leslie Cairns' shaggy eye-brows met in a ferocious scowl. "Don't be stingy. You won enough games last year. Have a heart!"

"Honestly, Les, you talk like an idiot!" exclaimed Natalie Weyman impatiently. "You have a crush, and no mistake, on that little Elster simpleton. I don't care whether you like what I say or not. You think she is a scream because she behaves more like a jockey than a student. I think she is so silly. You will get tired of her swaggering ways before long. See if you don't."

"She's a game little kid, and I like her," flung back Leslie with belligerent emphasis. "Why did you put me to all the trouble to fix things so that she could make the team if you didn't intend to give her a showing. That cost me time and money." Her voice rose harshly on the last words.

"Shh!" Dulcie Vale held up a warning finger. "You are almost shouting, Les. Lower your voice."

"I should *say* so." Natalie Weyman's face was a disagreeable study. Before the arrival of Lola Elster at Hamilton, she and Leslie had been intimate friends. Now Leslie had in a measure deserted her for the bold little freshman she so detested.

"Beg your pardon." Leslie's tones dropped back to their usual drawl. "Sorry you girls have decided you must break the record tomorrow. Why so strenuous? You haven't Beauty and her gang to fight. They haven't had even a look-in. I hear they are really *players*, too. The trouble with you, Nat, is you are two-faced. You pretended that you were anxious for Lola to make the team because you thought she would make a fine record for herself on the floor. You said her pals ought to be on the team, too. So they are, the three of them. I worked that. Now you didn't say that you wanted these three freshmen on the team so as to keep those Sanford upstarts off. I caught that, too, and fixed it. I didn't mind. I can't see them. What you wanted was a crowd of freshmen your team could whip easily."

"That is absolutely ridiculous and unkind in you,

Leslie!" Natalie's face was scarlet. "How could I possibly know beforehand just how well the freshmen we—that is—you——" Natalie stammered, then stopped.

Leslie Cairns' upper lip drew back in a sneering smile. "How could you know? Well, you dragged them over to the gym and set them at work with the ball. This was before the try-out. What? You took good care not to ask me along that day. Joan is as deep in it as you are. Then you came back puffing about what wonderful players these kids were and so forth. Would I fix it for them. I did. The day of the try-out I was pretty sore. You can't fool me on a basket ball. They are not much more than scrubs; except Lola. She is O. K. I saw you and Joan had put one over on me, but it was too late to make a fuss. Think I don't know you, Nat? Ah, but I do!"

Natalie sat biting her lip, her eyes narrowed. She was well aware that Leslie knew her traitorous disposition. For selfish reasons she did not wish to quarrel with her.

"All right, Leslie," she shrugged. "Have it your own way. Go on thinking that, if it will be any satisfaction to you. You must remember we have our own end to hold up as sophomores. Why, if we *tried* to favor Lola during the game, it would be noticed and we would have trouble over it.

Ever since that Beauty contest, I've noticed a difference in the way I am treated. I used to be *It* on the campus. I've lost ground, somehow. We Sans have worked too hard for first place here to give way now. We must keep up our popularity or be at the dictation of the common herd. Our team simply *has* to make good tomorrow."

CHAPTER XXII.

A HARD ASSIGNMENT.

WHEN the chimes rang out a melodious Angelus at six o'clock that evening, the sophomore-freshman game was over and the freshman had received the most complete whitewash on record at Hamilton. The score at the end of the game was 26-4 in favor of the sophs. In the freshman quarters, just off the main floor of the gymnasium, Lola Elster sat weeping tears of sheer fury, with Miss Cairns alone to comfort her.

"They told me they wouldn't work hard! They told me it would be a walk away!" she reiterated vengefully. "You wait. I'll be even with that Joan Myers!" The bulk of her spite was directed against Joan, with whom she had come most into contact during the game.

On the way to their respective campus houses, groups of indignant freshmen freely discussed and deplored the disgrace that had fallen upon them. At least thirty-five girls were bound for Silverton Hall, walking five abreast, their clear voices rising high in the energy of discussion. Among these were Marjorie, Ronny, Jerry and Lucy. All four were separated, each walking in a different group.

In the foremost rank were Robin Page, Portia Graham, Elaine Hunter, Blanche Scott and Marjorie. Four of them were engaged in trying to console Robina, who was feeling the disgrace keenly.

"You should have resigned from that team, Robin, the minute you saw what they were at practice," Blanche Scott said energetically. "It was fine in you to stick for the honor of the class. You did your best today, under the circumstances. You were the only one who scored."

"Yes; you need not feel bad, Robin," consoled Portia Graham. "I know one thing. There is going to be a new freshman team before long, and I hope you will play center."

"You believe, then, Portia, that we ought to raise a real fuss and demand a new team?" Elaine Hunter's blue eyes were alight with anticipation. She was glad to have some one else express her own thought.

"Yes; don't you? It is the only way to wipe our

escutcheon clear. Don't you agree with us, Miss
Dean? We should all stand together in a matter of
this kind. We can only guess as to why such a
team was picked in the first place. Good players
ignored and 'flunks' taken on, with the exception of
Robin. Miss Reid, I understand, favors a certain
element of students here. The management of the
sports is in her hands, but it should not be. It
really belongs to the senior sports committee. I
hear, that, for two or three years, they have been
positive figureheads. She has done all the managing. It is time there was a change."

"Two of the senior committee did not care much,
I believe. The manager, Miss Clement, told me
that she was simply over-ruled. She objected, but
that was all the good it did," informed Blanche
Scott.

Portia had gone on talking, without giving Marjorie a chance to agree with her. She now laughingly apologized and again solicited an opinion.

"I think a new team should be chosen," Marjorie
said evenly. Her eyes were sparkling in the darkness like twin stars. Here, at last, were girls like
the Lookouts. She was so glad that the matter was
to be taken up and threshed out she could have
shouted. A definite blow for democracy was about
to be struck at Hamilton. "My friends and I
thought the try-out very unfair. We are considered

good players at home, but we were not even chosen to sub."

She went on a little further to explain why, in her estimation, the team chosen were so unfit for the responsibility. Her short talk proved conclusively that she understood basket ball as only an expert could.

"Won't you and Miss Harding please enter the lists again, when we have the new try-out?" coaxed Elaine Hunter.

'No." Marjorie's refusal was quietly emphatic. "Not this year. I am willing to do all I can to help the good work along, but I don't care to play. Muriel feels the same. Next year we hope to make the team. There are some good players among the freshmen who had no chance at the try-out. I would like to see them play. I would like to see Miss Page play center. She plays a wonderful game."

"Thank you." Walking beside Marjorie, Robin gave her arm a grateful little squeeze. "You and I are going to be great friends," she laughed. "How did you guess my pet ambition?"

"I didn't guess it. I only said what I thought about it. You deserve the position."

"Yes; and she is going to have it, if there is any such thing as fair play at Hamilton, and I think there is." Portia Graham spoke with a sternness that presaged action. "After dinner, tonight, I am going to call a meeting in the back parlor. We can all get into that room without crowding. Then we will see what happens." True to her word, Portia saw to it, the moment she reached the Hall, that every freshman in the house was notified of the meeting.

The ringing of the dinner gong shortly afterward was a pleasing sound to the hungry girls. Dinner at Silverton Hall was served at two long tables set lengthwise in a pretty green and white dining room. The Lookouts found the meal as appetizing as any they had eaten at Wayland Hall, though no better. They liked the line-up of merry girls, with most of whom they now had some acquaintance.

Dessert did not receive its usual attention that night. The excited freshmen finished their dinners in some haste and promptly repaired to the back parlor. The same thirty-five who had walked five abreast across the campus were gathered again for action. While the murmur of conversation, mingled with frequent laughter, went on until Portia Graham took up her station near the old-fashioned fireplace where she could be seen and heard. Immediately the buzzing subsided, to be succeeded by a total silence.

Her freshman honor stung by the whitewashing the freshman team had received, she made an address that came straight from her injured feelings.

It was not long, but it was convincing and evoked loud approbation. Her suggestion was that a letter of protest be written to Miss Reid and signed by every freshman in sympathy with the movement.

"That excludes four members of the team and a few of their supporters, but we can't help that," she said. "I think a committee of three had best draw up the letter. Then it can be passed around for approval and signatures. Be very sure to read it carefully. This letter is going to make Miss Reid very angry, for she will have to know that we considered her methods unfair. I do not believe she will take up the matter with Doctor Matthews. If she should, we will stand our ground. We are going to stamp out favoritism if we can. After the letter leaves here with our signatures it will be handed to the freshmen at Acasia House. I will obtain their signatures. There are six at Wayland Hall and all are in sympathy. That leaves about twenty-four, including the team. The majority of the twenty besides the team are doubtful. Elaine, I am going to ask you and Miss Dean if you will accept the delicate task of obtaining the signatures of any of the twenty whom you think are with us."

"I will do the best I can. That is no simple undertaing, Portia Graham," Elaine reminded, her gentle face rather blank at the mission. Marjorie also looked a trifle anxious. Then her face cleared and she expressed her willingness to comply with Portia's request.

Jerry's lips puckered as though about to emit a whistle when she heard Portia commission the two freshmen to the difficult task. She was about to set Portia hastily down in her mind as on the order of a shirker. She had passed the hardest task to some one else. Then it suddenly dawned upon her that, among the freshmen, there were no two better able to diplomatically perform that task than Marjorie and Elaine.

CHAPTER XXIII.

A FRESHMAN REVOLT.

The committee of three, which included Portia Graham, Veronica and Ethel Laird, an Acasia House freshman, duly met on the following evening. After two hours of good hard work they succeeded in preparing a letter of protest which suited them. It was a drastic letter, written out of the adamant hardness of youth against injustice. The Silverton Hall freshmen hailed it with acclamation and vowed that it ought to be placed on record with the world's great documents. The Acasia House contingent were no less enthusiastic. There were

twenty of them, which, with the six at Wayland
Hall, swelled the number of protestants to fifty-
eight. This represented two-thirds of the class.

It was a week from the time the letter was written and copied before it was signed by the loyal two-
thirds. Portia made haste prudently, never allowing the precious document to be out of her sight
during the signing process. Each freshman was
also pledged not to mention it outside the class.
During that period of time, Marjorie and Elaine
were carefully scouting about for signers among the
doubtful contingent. It was indeed a hard detail.

She and Elaine made a list of the names of the
twenty doubtfuls and divided it between them.
That made only ten apiece, but, oh, that ten! She
finally managed by dint of inquiry to obtain three
signatures from three girls who lived off the campus
and did their own light house-keeping. They appeared to be pleased with her call, which she made
one snowy December afternoon, and became willing
signers. She promptly told Ronny of them, who as
promptly pricked up her ears. These were the very
girls Ronny was always ready to help. This
brought her list down to seven. Five of these she
learned were devoted supporters of Lola Elster.
Thus, only two of her original ten were left. One
of these two was a Miss Savage, who lived at
Alston Terrace, the most distant house from Hamil-

ton Hall on the campus. She roomed with her sister, a junior, and recited French in Marjorie's class.
The other, a Miss Greene, Marjorie knew only by
sight. She lived in the town of Hamilton and a
chauffeur brought her and came for her with a
limousine every afternoon.

How to get in touch with them she did not know.
She was certain that Leila Harper could help her in
this, but she was under promise of silence. The
freshmen signers were growing a trifle impatient, as
they wished to have the affair out of the way before
going home for Christmas. Elaine had secured six
of her ten signatures. The other four she reported
as hopeless. She volunteered to see Miss Savage,
whom she had met socially on several occasions.

"I don't believe I will be able to get that Miss
Greene's signature," Marjorie confided to Ronny.
"I am never anywhere near her. I never see her
with any of the Sans or Miss Elster's friends. She
is not chummy with them. Still, I dislike going up
to her and asking her to sign when I don't know
her even to bow to."

"I would not trouble myself about her," advised
Ronny. "I do not like her looks. I heard, quite a
while ago, that she was very distant. It is too bad
you had to bother with that list. Still, I would have
accepted it had I been asked to do so. The end is
worth the pains in this case."

Marjorie nodded. "Oh, I didn't much mind. I am glad I slid through without any fussing. Right is right, only one can't always make the other person see it. I will go over to Silverton Hall today after classes and tell Portia I can't get hold of Miss Greene. Perhaps she can."

Shortly after four that afternoon, Marjorie walked slowly down the main drive, intending presently to strike off across the campus in the direction of Silverton Hall. She had not gone far when she heard the crunch of a footstep behind her. Involuntarily she turned her head to encounter the cold stare of two pale blue eyes. "Oh!" was her soft-breathed interjection. The eyes belonged to Miss Greene. More, Miss Greene was about to address her.

"Are you Miss Dean, the young woman who is getting signatures for a protest against Miss Reid's management of basket ball?" she asked icily.

"Yes," Marjorie unhesitatingly answered, measuring the questioner with a calm, uncritical glance. "I have not your signature. Do you wish to sign the paper we shall presently send Miss Reid?"

"Where is this paper?" counter-questioned Miss Greene. "I wish to see it. I have never heard of anything more outrageous! Miss Reid is a dear friend of mine."

Marjorie colored hotly at the other's tone. Raising her head she coolly stared Miss Greene straight in the eye. "I have not the paper with me. In any case you would not care to sign it. It is in the form of a letter to Miss Reid and is just. The outrageous part of the affair lies in Miss Reid having shown favoritism, not in the freshmen having resented it. Good afternoon." She continued on down the drive, leaving an angry freshman behind her.

Portia Graham received the account of the interview with troubled eyes. "Who do you suppose told her?" she asked Marjorie. "We were anxious to send the letter before news of it reached Miss Reid. She deserves it, you know. My sister graduated from here last June and she could not endure Miss Reid. Of course, Miss Greene will tell her, if she hasn't already. We had best send the letter at once. A little early for a Christmas greeting, but it will give her food for reflection," Portia finished sarcastically.

"There are no games to be played before Christmas, anyway," returned Marjorie. "What we wish to prevent is another exhibition of how not to play basket ball as given by that limping team. Suppose Miss Reid ignores our letter?"

"Then we will take it higher," was the quick response. "She won't. She will probably send for the committee which I informed her in the letter

would meet her to discuss the matter. I did not
mention any names. Will you go with me if she
sends for us? I would like Miss Lynne and Miss
Harding, Elaine and Miss Cornell."

"I will go and so will Ronny and Muriel." Marjorie gave the promise for herself and friends.

Miss Greene now out of the question, and Elaine
having obtained Miss Savage's signature, there was
no further time wasted. The letter was sent and
the freshmen rested their case until a reply came.
Reply, however, was not forthcoming. Up to the
day when college closed for the Christmas holidays
Miss Reid had made no sign save to haughtily
ignore the justice-seeking freshmen when she encountered them on the campus. The six girls, who
formed the committee for final action, quietly
agreed that as soon as they returned from their
holiday vacation they would immediately wait upon
Miss Reid and demand justice.

Occupied with this matter, Marjorie had allowed
her own affairs to slide for a time. The day before
going home, she recalled with regret that she had
intended to invite Leila Harper to spend the holidays with her. It was too late now. Still, there
would be the Easter vacation. She would invite
Leila for that, before going home. Leila's bright
blue eyes filled with tears when Marjorie delivered
her invitation.

"You are a darling," she said unsteadily. "I would accept in a minute, but I am going home with Vera. Easter, now you have asked me, I will accept with loud Irish rejoicing. Vera is almost as much of a stray as I. Her father is Roderick Mason, the portrait painter. They have a whopping old apartment in the Glendenning, on Central Park, west. It is part studio. Her mother died when she was three weeks old. Her father brought her up. He's a fine man, but erratic. Whatever she asks him for he says: 'Yes, yes; but don't annoy me with it.' He loves her when he happens to recall that he has a daughter," Leila ended half bitterly.

"I wish Vera would spend Easter with us, too," Marjorie said quickly. "I shall invite her before I go home. Come along. We will ask her now. I am going home on that eight-ten train in the morning, so I won't have time then to see her."

Leila's face was aglow with a new-found happiness as she and Marjorie ran up the stairs to Vera's room. There was that in Marjorie's sweet cordiality which thawed the ice about her heart. Next to Vera, she had received Marjorie into her affections. In consequence, she was more in touch with Marjorie's college affairs then the latter dreamed. Leila was in possession of the news of the freshman revolt against Miss Reid, but she kept it strictly to herself. She also honored Marjorie and her chums for being able to keep a secret. The news, in reality, had been published abroad by Miss Reid herself, who had showed the letter to Natalie Weyman, Leslie Cairns and even Lola Elster. These three had been furiously angry over the attempt to "put one over," as Leslie Cairns had expressed herself.

"Let it go until we come back from our vacation. Don't see any of them," she stolidly advised Miss Reid. "I will find a way to settle them. Lola stays on the team. I heard this Miss Dean, Beauty, you know," she sneered, "was trotting around with the paper. I know a way to even up scores with her. Leave it to me. Oh, yes. I'll tell you one thing you may do. Write that snippy Miss Page and demand her resignation from the team. That will make the revolutionists wild. As soon as we come back make the freshies challenge us to play. I'll see that they win next time and don't you flunk, either. The soph's team will have to do as I say. They all owe me money."

Miss Reid entertained great respect for the Cairns money, though at heart she was not fond of Leslie and her bullying ways. She was obliged to admit that Leslie Cairns was a born politician. This was not strange. Her father was Peter Cairns, the hardest-headed tyrant among a group of financiers who based all values on money.

"I believe you are right, Leslie, about the freshman team challenging the sophomore team directly after the holidays," she reluctantly conceded. "If the freshman team should win, it would put a stop to this nonsense. I shall put a stop to it, at any rate, by simply ignoring it." Miss Reid was carefully ignoring all recognition of the fact that Leslie had the upper hand and was dictating to her. This fact was not lost on Leslie.

"The freshman team must win," she said, looking hard at the physical instructor. "If you can't manage it, I will send for a coach who can. I can have him here for two weeks before the game. He can live in town and I'll run him out here in my car every day to coach the team. I don't mean Fulton. He is too namby-pamby. I mean a coach who will really train the team and at the same time keep off any freshmen who start to interfere."

"That will not be necessary, Leslie." Miss Reid's tones were freighted with annoyance. "I believe I can be trusted to coach the freshman team so that they will—well, make a good showing at the next game."

"Win the game?" was the significant question.

"Yes, win the game," repeated Miss Reid. "Please recall that I selected that team; not the coach. It doesn't include any of your pet aversions. I hope I am equal to this emergency."

"I hope so," returned Lesile, without enthusiasm.

"Anyway, I shall keep an eye on the team myself.
Now if Nat comes raving to you about Lola or me
pay no attention to her. She wants to be a basket
ball star and it's an inconvenient time to aspire to
it. Understand? What?" With this final char-
acteristic interjection, Leslie sauntered out of the
instructor's room without troubling to say good-bye.
It had not occurred to her to say "Merry Christmas" or wish Miss Reid the season's compliments,
although the conversation took place between them
not more than two hours before Leslie left Hamilton to go to New York for the holidays.

Happily unconscious of any dark conspiracies
against her welfare, Marjorie's last night at the
Hall was congenially spent. The Five Travelers
had packed in the afternoon and were free to spend
the evening together. They had decided to use the
time in wrapping and directing a number of pack-
ages, containing simple remembrances for a few of
the Hamilton students whose home addresses they
had secured. These they could mail at the station
the next morning. While the five girls talked and
worked, their old friend, the chimes, entertained
them with his ever beautiful Christmas repertoire.
"Hark the Herald Angels Sing," "Silent Night,"
"Little Town of Bethlehem," "Cheerful Adoration,"
and other Yuletide favorites rang gloriously out on
the still snowy air. The concert ended with "God

Rest You, Merry Gentlemen," which had been Brooke Hamilton's pet carol.

"Thank you ever so much, old dear," Marjorie made a childish little bow in the direction of her friend as the little prelude before the striking of eleven began. The ten-thirty rule was not being observed that night and no one cared.

"Yes; much obliged chimes," echoed Jerry. "It will be quite awhile before we hear your melodious voice again. There, that's my last package." She laid an oblong bundle on a pile beside her with an audible sigh of satisfaction.

"Mine, too. Come on, Lucy, we must turn in. Shoo, shoo, Muriel. Go right straight to your room. It's late. Didn't you know it." Ronny made a playful attempt to drive Muriel to the door. The latter braced her feet and stood her ground. Both girls were laughing as were also the three on-lookers. The sound of mirth could be faintly heard in the hall.

Coming in from a motor ride with several of the Sans, Natalie Weyman heard the laughter as she passed Marjorie's room on the way to her own. Her face clouded perceptibly. What a lot those girls seemed to find to laugh at, was her resentful thought. She was always hearing sounds of laughter from both Marjorie's room and that of her friend across the hall. It was evident they did not quarrel much. For an instant Natalie wished she knew them better. Leslie and Dulcie were always so disagreeable unless they could have their own way. Remembering her grudge against Marjorie, her lips tightened. What she really wished was not to know Marjorie better; only to be even with her for what she considered an irreparable injury done her.

CHAPTER XXIV.

THE FIRST VICTORY.

After two weeks of undiluted happiness at home, Marjorie's return to Hamilton was a wrench, keenly felt by all immediately concerned. According to her own ideas it was like a plant; nicely rooted in one soil, only to be jerked up by the roots and transplanted. Once returned to Wayland Hall, it took her longer to settle down than at Thanksgiving. She had little spells of yearning for her father and mother which only time dimmed.

For a week following the return of the Five Travelers to Hamilton, they heard nothing of basket ball interests save that Miss Reid had still made no reply to the letter sent her. Another week passed, during which the fall term ended and two days of written tests ensued. Then came one day of vacation which was always given the students of Hamilton at the closing of a term. It was on the afternoon of this holiday that the freshman class, minus fourteen members, who had purposely been left out, met in the living room of Silverton Hall. It was a tight squeeze, but every one of the sixty-eight girls managed to crowd into the room. Portia Graham stood on a chair backed against the wall to address them. When she had finished speaking the room rang with cheers. She had advocated a committee to wait on Miss Reid and insist on fair treatment.

"In the event that Miss Reid refuses us justice, are you in favor of taking our grievance higher?" she questioned in purposeful tones.

"YES!" was the unanimous shout.

"Contrary?" she inquired sweetly, but there were no contrary members present.

"Are you satisfied with the choice of the following members as a committee? Their names are: Veronica Lynne, Marjorie Dean, Muriel Harding, Elaine Hunter, Mary Cornell, Portia Graham."

Another resounding affirmative, followed by no dissenting voices, was immediately forthcoming.

"That settles it," she declared grimly. "We will call on Miss Reid tomorrow evening at eight o'clock. For the benefit of any one not yet familiar

with Hamilton, I will say that Miss Reid lives at
Randolph House. If she is not in, we will make
another call on the next evening. I ask you on your
honor as freshmen of 19— not to speak of this to
anyone after you leave here."

At ten minutes to eight the next evening the
committee met in front of Wayland Hall and proceeded across the campus toward the north to Randolph House which was devoted to faculty. They
walked briskly along on the frozen lawn, almost in
silence. Portia was to be spokesman, and she was
mentally framing her remarks as she went. She
was not in the least diffident when it came to facing
Miss Reid, and she intended to drive home her
point.

The assurance of the maid who answered their
ring that Miss Reid was in, sent a queer little thrill
over them all. Marjorie smiled to herself as she
entered the reception room. This was not the first
disagreeable call she had been obliged by duty to
make.

A ten minutes' wait, during which they con-
versed a little in low tones, and Miss Reid appeared.
She was a tall woman, rather attractive at first
glance, but not as one studied her features. Her
small black eyes were shrewd and furtive, while the
expression of her full face in repose was self-satis-
fied rather than agreeable.

"Good evening," she saluted, in an uninterested tone. She looked from one to another of her visitors as though nonplussed by the invasion. Both tone and look were intended to deceive. Miss Reid guessed the nature of the call.

"Good evening," was the united salutation. The committee viewed the instructor with a gravity which nettled her.

"We called this evening, Miss Reid," Portia began sternly, "because you have paid no attention to the letter we sent you before the holidays. It was signed by more than two-thirds of the freshman class and merited a reply which you did not make. We were serious in our intent, and expected you would treat our complaint with traditional courtesy. You did not. We have, therefore, come here to ask you if you intend to grant us the justice of a new team."

"Certainly not." A tide of dull color had risen to Miss Reid's face as she listened to Portia's blunt arraignment. Her eyes had begun to snap and her pronounced black brows were drawn together. "You are insolent, Miss Graham. I simply will not discuss the matter with you. I will say only that the present team remains, with the exception of Miss Page. I have requested her resignation. Her team-mates complain she is not fast enough for the work. I mailed her a note this afternoon. You

must understand that you cannot fly in the face of
a member of the faculty and hope to gain by such
an act. I am amazed at freshman—we will say
—temerity."

A sinister stillness followed Miss Reid's caustic
retaliation. A battery of scornful eyes was leveled
at the disgruntled instructor. The very air was
thick with the committee's displeasure. This latest
piece of injustice, directed against Robin Page,
capped the climax. It was two minutes, at least,
before Portia could trust her voice in a reply. She
was angry enough to wrathfully denounce Miss
Reid, then and there.

"It will not be necessary for Miss Page to resign
from the team. She has already been sufficiently
humiliated by having been identified with a set of
scrub players. There will be a new freshman team
and Miss Page will play on it. I am certain that
Doctor Matthews will understand that something
of unusual unfairness has happened to stir the
majority of the freshman class into revolt." Every
word Portia uttered cut clearly on the stillness of
the room.

"Oh, not the majority of the freshman class, Miss
Graham." Miss Reid's intonation was that of one
correcting a glaring exaggeration. It was accompanied by a smile of malicious incredulity.

"If you will refer to the letter sent you before

the holidays, you will find that it was signed by sixty-eight freshmen. The class numbers eighty-two. A meeting of the sixty-eight freshmen who resent your unfairness was called yesterday. The result—we are here tonight." Portia's retort was laden with cold, uncompromising dignity.

It was distinctly chilling to the physical instructor's audacious stand. For the first time since her entrance into the room she became ill at ease. The force with which she had to deal was altogether too active for comfort. She knew that Portia would keep her word. With sixty-eight incensed freshmen at her back, Doctor Matthews would not only listen but investigate. An investigation would be decidedly humiliating to her, and also jeopardize her position at Hamilton. She found herself caught between two fires. She had promised Leslie Cairns that Lola Elster's team would win. It would not be easy to pacify Leslie if she acceded to the committee's demand. Self-preservation must be considered first, however. After the high hand she had just taken in answering Portia, she hardly knew what to say.

"I— that is ——" she began, stopped, then said with as much of an attempt at offended dignity as she could muster: "I cannot talk further with you concerning this matter tonight. I have an engagement with two members of the faculty and am already late. If you will come to the gymnasium at four o'clock tomorrow afternoon I will see what I can do to pacify the freshman class. I would prefer resigning all interest in basket ball rather than be the center of a freshman quarrel." She rose from her chair, as though determined to end the uncomfortable interview.

"Very well," Portia coldly inclined her head. "We shall expect to see you in the gymnasium at four o'clock. We will not detain you longer."

She rose. Her companions immediately followed suit. Portia's "good evening" was echoed by the others as they filed through the door, their soft, young faces set in cold contempt.

Not a word passed among them until they were well away from the house. Elaine Hunter was the first to speak. "Did you ever see anyone more upset than Miss Reid was toward the last?" she asked her companions in general.

"She had good reason to be," returned Portia grimly. "We have won our point. I hope she does resign basket ball management. A senior told me recently that she has always been a bugbear to the teams. She insists on managing everything and everybody who will let her. Miss Reid has had the reputation for years of favoring money and fighting principle. She has repeatedly used basket ball favors as means of ingratiating herself with wealthy students. If she really makes good what she said about resigning it will be the first important victory for democracy at Hamilton."

CHAPTER XXV.

A NEW CONSPIRACY.

NOT daring to break the appointment she had made with the freshman committee, Miss Reid met them the next afternoon in the gymnasium at the time she had set. She had been very careful, in the meantime, not to come in contact with Leslie Cairns or Lola Elster. Deep in her soul, she was raging at the choice which had been forced upon her. Fear of losing her position of years' standing at Hamilton, and the even more active fear that perhaps her connivance with Leslie Cairns was known in college, urged her to shun campus publicity. Resignation was the one way out of her difficulties with both parties. It would check all freshman activities against her. As for Leslie, what could she say or do in the face of it? She would be angry, of course, and insulting. Insults, however, broke no bones. Leslie could not circulate malicious reports about her without implicating herself. To resign also meant a saving of dignity. Miss Reid determined, therefore, to resign, but without appointing a time for a new try-out. She would slide from under and let the freshmen straighten the snarl as best they might.

A plan is not a success until it has been carried out. This Miss Reid learned at her second interview with the committee. Portia, backed by the other members of the committee, insisted that Miss Reid should sign a notice of her own composition, announcing a new try-out.

"You may say, if you choose, that, owing to the dissatisfaction of the preponderance of the freshman class with the work of the present basket ball team, you have been requested by a committee, representing freshman interests, to call another try-out for the purpose of selecting another team, composed of players, adequate to the work."

"But no such thing has ever been heard of, much less done, here at Hamilton," objected Miss Reid, when Portia coolly outlined the notice.

"It has been heard of now and must be done," came the instant answer. "I assure you, Miss Reid, that you will go further toward gaining the respect of the students by being impersonal in this affair. You have been severely criticized for allowing so inadequate a team to take the floor. On the day of the first try-out good players were ignored and unskilful ones chosen. You will gain more by rectifying this error. You owe it to yourself to do so before you resign. We freshmen prefer the seniors as managers of our college sports. You have not been just with us and we have resented your injustice."

Portia's denunciation of the physical instructor's methods was, undoubtedly, candid. It had the desired effect, however. Miss Reid wrote and posted the notice. Further, she sent a frigid little note to the senior manager of college sports, whom she had treated so discourteously on the day of the try-out, renouncing all voice and interest in basket ball.

The victorious committee's next move was to get in touch with the senior sports committee of three, which included Miss Clement, the senior manager, and notify them of the complete revolution of affairs. The two who had sided with Miss Reid agreed quite meekly now with the committee's ideas. The try-out was held in the gymnasium shortly after the notice had been posted, and, for once, a team was made up on its merits. Robin Page again made good and won the coveted position of center. The request for her resignation from the other team had not specially troubled Robin, knowing that a shake-up was imminent.

Four released and exasperated freshmen, headed by Lola Elster and reinforced by the ten classmates

in sympathy with the ex-team besieged Miss Reid,
demanding re-instatement. She very quickly thrust
the burden on the shoulders of the senior sports
committee. She made it plain to her favorites, also,
just who was responsible for the affair. As they
had no case they dared not take their grievance
higher. What they proceeded to do was seek the
consolation of the Sans, all fourteen of them being
at least eligible to association with these exclusives.
Their domineering sophomore sisters obligingly
promised them vengeance against the obnoxious
committee.

Leslie Cairns' receipt of the movement against
collusion was a fit of temper such as she seldom
gave way to. Spying the notice on the bulletin
board, she deliberately ripped it off and tore it to
bits. Then she set off for the gymnasium at a pace
quite foreign to her usual leisurely gait. Luckily
for Miss Reid, she happened to be elsewhere at the
time. Thus, when she and Leslie came to classes
on the following afternoon, the latter had calmed
considerably. She did not spare the older woman's
feelings, but scored her sharply for "bungling" and
then leaving her friends in the lurch in order to
save herself.

"You may say what you please, Leslie, but it
would have done no good to defy them," the instructor defended. "The freshman class this year

is a collection of young anarchists. I would advise you to be very careful what you do. There has not been such a class in years at Hamilton. A few more like it and Hamilton will lose its reputation as a really exclusive college."

"What Hamilton ought to lose is some of its freshie freshmen," retorted Leslie. "I have a friend who knows a lot about one of them, at least, and she probably knows enough about some others to queer them here. I mean those ninnies from that little one-horse town of Sanford. The whole five of them are an eyesore to me. The only one who hates 'em harder than I do, is Nat. She never will forgive that moon-eyed Miss Dean for putting it over her at the Beauty contest. Leila Harper was back of that. She is another I could see leave Hamilton without going into mourning."

"You can place the blame upon the Silverton Hall crowd, with Miss Graham and Miss Page as ringleaders," informed Miss Reid sourly.

Leslie shrugged sceptically. "Oh, I don't know," she differed. "Nat thinks Miss Dean's crowd started it. They took up the cudgels for that dig, Miss Langly. The minute we started to rag her for being so bull-headed about her room, this crowd of sillies started in rooting for her. Now old Proffy Wenderblatt and his family have taken her up and they make a fuss over her. She and the green-eyed

Sanford dig are *so chummy.* They make me sick. We have to be careful now about ragging her. Wenderblatt is a terror when he isn't pleased. He would report us to Doctor Matthews. Ragging is forbidden here, same as hazing. I'd do both to any one I didn't like, if I thought I could get away with it."

Despite Leslie Cairns' threats, made not only to Miss Reid but to Natalie Weyman and a few others, life slid along very peacefully for the Five Travelers. The holidays past, they found enjoyment in settling down for the winter term to uninterrupted study, lightened by impromptu social gatherings, held in one another's rooms. Occasionally they made dinner engagements at Silverton or Acasia House or entertained at Baretti's, their favorite haunt when in search of good cheer. Once a week they spent an hour together as the Five Travelers, and found the little confidential session helpful. No misunderstandings had crept in among them. Often their talks branched off into impersonalities, of interest to all.

Neither Marjorie nor Muriel had entered the second basket ball try-out. Both had decided to wait until their sophomore year. Fond of the game, they dropped into the gymnasium occasionally for an hour's work with the ball by way of keeping up practice. There were always plenty of subs willing to make up a team.

February came, bringing with it St. Valentine's day, and the masque which the juniors always gave on St. Valentine's night. A Valentine post box was one of the features. For days beforehand the girls spent odd moments in making valentines, the rule being that all valentines posted must have been hand wrought. Marjorie, remembering the cunning little-girl costume Mary Raymond had worn to Mignon La Salle's fancy dress party, shortened a frilled pink organdie gown of hers and went back to childhood for a night. With pink flat-heeled kid slippers and pink silk stockings, an immense pink top-knot bow tying up a portion of her curls, she was a pretty sight. Ronny went as a Watteau shepherdess, Lucy as a Japanese girl, Muriel as Rosalind in Shakespeare's "As You Like It," and Jerry as a clown.

The valentine party was always a delightful feature of the college year, for the reason that it was a masquerade. Though the Sans had been holding themselves rigidly aloof from all but a few students since the downfall of Lola Elster as a basket ball star, they could not resist the lure of a masquerade. They took good care to keep together until after the unmasking, presumably for fear of mingling with what they considered as "the common herd."

"Anyone with a good pair of keen eyes can tell the precious Sans though they should be happening to wear a dozen masks," Leila Harper had derided. "They wear such silks and satins and velvets and jewels! They are wearying to the sight with their fine clothes. Look at me. A poor Irish colleen with nothing silk about me but one small neckerchief."

Following the masquerade by only a few days came the excitement of the first game between the new team and the sophomores. The latter had not challenged the freshman team after its reorganization, as Leslie Cairns had voiced against it and neither Natalie nor Joan Meyers cared to oppose her. Leslie possessed a very large fortune in her own right. In consequence she always had money in abundance. While the former had large allowances, they managed usually to overstep them. In such case they fell back on Leslie and were invariably in her debt.

Later Leslie changed her mind about not wishing the sophomores to play against the "upstarts," as she termed them. Having overheard on the campus that the sophs were afraid to meet the freshies, she accordingly urged Joan to challenge the freshman team.

When the game came off on the third Saturday in February, the freshmen gave the sophomores a drubbing they would not soon forget. It was not a whitewash, but it was painfully near it. The sophomore players took the defeat with very poor grace. The freshman class had gone wild when the game had ended 26-10 in favor of the freshmen. While the sophs had not expected a walk-away victory, they had confidently expected to win. Further, Leslie had promised them a dinner at Baretti's that should outdo anything she had given that year. Now that they had lost the game, she obstinately refused to keep her word.

"Why spend my good money on a crowd of no accounts like you?" she had roughly queried. "I said if you *won* I'd give the dinner. You did not, so what's the use in celebrating. The fault with you girls is you've been slackers about practicing. You've gone motoring when you should have been in the gym and after the ball." This rebuke was delivered in the sophs' dressing room after the game, whence the team had hurried to hide their diminished heads.

"Do you know what I heard out on the floor?" she continued, with intent to hurt. "I heard that the sophs might have won if they had practiced once in a while."

"Just the same the freshies had coaching all the

time and we didn't," Dulcie Vale asserted. "Miss Dean and Miss Harding are both expert players. It seems that they play basket ball a lot at these high schools. These girls get to be very clever at it. Like the Indians, you know, who make such good foot ball players. They showed the team different plays to use against us. That's why they won. They have been over to the gym almost every day."

Dulcie's comparison of Muriel and Marjorie to the Indians raised a laugh, as she intended it should. Even Leslie laughed in her peculiar silent fashion. Next instant she frowned. She had again been thwarted by the girls she despised. Things were not going rightly at all. Born a bully, she looked upon even her friends as created only for her amusement. She had the insatiable desire for power, and could not bear defeat. Tucked in an inner pocket of her tweed top coat was a letter she had recently received. It was not the first one she had received from the same source. This particular letter had appeared to afford her great satisfaction on reading. Her hand strayed to the pocket which held it.

"I have a letter here I would like to read to you girls," she drawled. "On second thoughts I'll take back what I said. I'll stand for that blowout at Baretti's. That would be a good place to read you the letter. Then I would like your advice on it."

CHAPTER XXVI.

FRIENDS GOOD AND TRUE.

"Do you see anything about me to laugh at?" demanded Marjorie one snowy afternoon in early March, as she walked into her room, eyes sparkling, cheeks aglow, not only from the winter air, but from annoyance as well.

Jerry looked up from an illustrated magazine she was interestedly perusing. "No; I don't. I'll laugh if you say so. Ha, ha! Ha, ha!" This obligingly and without a smile.

"You needn't mind. That laugh of yours has a hollow sound. It's not what I would call true mirth."

"No wonder it has a hollow sound. I'm hungry," Jerry complained. "It is almost an hour until dinner, too. Tell me what's bothering you. It will take my mind off my hungry self."

"Oh, nothing startling, only every time I meet any of the Sans or those few freshmen who go around with them, they look me all over and then they do everything from smiling just the least bit, a hateful sarcastic smile, to laughing outright. Just now, as I came across the campus, I met Miss Cairns. Miss Elster, Miss Myers and Miss Weyman were with her. As soon as they saw me, they began to talk among themselves, quite loudly. I didn't hear what they said. I know it was about me. Then they all laughed. The other day I met the same girls and they simply smiled. I know they are doing it purposely; but why?"

"Humph!" ejaculated Jerry, her blue eyes widening in sudden belligerence. "I know why! They have started out to rag you. That's a nice proposition! I suppose they are sore at you because you were on that committee."

"But that was quite a while ago. This making fun of me has only been of late. I noticed it first the Sunday after the game. I met a crowd of those girls as I came from chapel. I felt just a little hurt. I had had such a peaceful time in chapel. It was the Sunday you had a cold and did not attend chapel. If they keep it up, I shall probably grow so used to it that it won't trouble me."

"Well, if they confine themselves to snickering, smirking, ha-ha-ing and te-he-ing, let 'em enjoy themselves. If they start to say anything to you, for that's the next stage in ragging, give them *one lovely* call-down that will settle them for good. You can do it. I've heard you speak straight from the shoulder. Will you ever forget the day you and I had the fuss with Row-ena Fightena Quarrelena Scrapena?"

"No; I will not." Marjorie never could resist giggling at the long name which Jerry had applied to Rowena Farnham on account of the latter's quarrelsome disposition. "I hope none of those Sans will try her tactics. I don't wish to come to bitter words with any of those girls. They are set against me on account of having served on that committee, perhaps. Maybe because Muriel and I went over to the gym occasionally and helped the team along. They have not liked us, you know, from the night Miss Cairns, Miss Weyman and Miss Vale called and privately rated us as nobodies. It is queer they never tried to take Ronny up, for she has made no secret of her name this year. They must surely have heard of Alfred Lynne, her father. Leila says that Miss Cairns is always writing her father and asking him to have this or that student's parents looked up financially."

"Contemptible!" Jerry's scorn of such tactics was sweeping. "If ever they try to look me up and I hear of it, even long afterward, I will get them together and give them such a call-down their hair will stand on end and stay that way for a week. If you should happen to see the Sans switching around the campus with their coiffures resembling that of Feejee Islanders, you will know what has occurred to the dear creatures. I shall probably do that, anyhow, if they don't let you alone."

"No." Marjorie's negative was decided. "You must never fuss with them on my account. I daresay they will grow tired before long of making fun of me. All I can do is this. Appear not to see them at all."

"I would just as soon fuss with them as look at them," Jerry declared valorously. "Now who are they, pray tell me? One thing is certain to come to pass. Sooner or later we will have to tell that crowd where they get off at. I have seen it coming ever since the freshman dance. Miss Weyman is so mad at you she can't see straight. She expected to win that contest. Helen Trent called my attention to her that night. She was posing to beat the band for the judges' benefit. Helen was worried a little. She thought Leila ought not to have pitted you against Miss Weyman. That is what she did, you know. Afterward Helen said she guessed you would have been unofficially declared the college beauty anyway, for so many of the girls were already raving over you. Now don't rave at me for telling you that. You are such an old sorehead about that contest. I hardly dare think of it in the same room with you."

Marjorie sat very still, an expression of blank

amazement on her lovely face. She now recalled
her own vexation on the night of the dance when
Leila had brought her into too prominent notice by
hurrying her across one end of the gymnasium to
join the line. So Leila had purposely dragged her
into that contest! For a moment or two she wav-
ered on the verge of indignation at Leila. Then the
Irish girl's face, brooding and wistful, as she had
seen it so many times when Leila was referring to
her own affairs, rose before her. No; it was too
late to be angry with Leila. Marjorie was tempted
to laugh instead at the clever way in which Leila
had managed the whole affair.

"You have told me some news," she said at last.
"I had no idea Miss Weyman was anxious to win
the contest. I didn't know, either, that Leila had
a hand in it. She didn't say much about it after it
was over, except to congratulate me. I don't think
she has ever mentioned it since." Marjorie had
begun to smile.

"She is a clever one." Jerry grinned apprecia-
tion of the absent Leila. "Why, Marjorie, she
arranged that contest! She took it from an old
book on the Celts. She brought the book with her
from Ireland. She got up the contest to score one
against the Sans and take a rise out of Miss Weyman. I would have told you this before, but Helen
told me in confidence. She said the other day she

didn't care if I told you, for she felt that you understood Leila well enough now not to be cross with
her. She was afraid of making trouble in the
beginning if she said anything."

"It's past now. I don't care. Miss Weyman is
nothing to me. I am glad I know about it, though."
Marjorie considered for a brief space. "Perhaps
that is why those girls are acting so queerly toward
me. They may think me very much elated over
winning the contest. If that's the case, all the more
reason why I should pay no attention to them."

Jerry agreed that this was so and the subject was
dropped for the time being. Having resolved to
appear oblivious to any ill-bred acts on the part of
the Sans, Marjorie proceeded to carry out her resolution. For a week or more she presented a
strictly impersonal face whenever she chanced to
encounter any of the Sans or their friends in going
about the college premises. She was greatly annoyed to find that this method seemed to have no
effect. Instead, their derision of herself was growing more pronounced. Several times she thought
she detected a difference in the salutations of certain upper class students who had formerly shown
cordiality of greeting. Late one afternoon she met
Miss Kingston, one of the seniors on the sports
committee, on the steps of the library, and received
from her merely a blank stare. Marjorie went on

to the Hall, feeling very much crushed. To be sure she was not particularly interested in Miss Kingston. She had sided with Miss Reid at the try-out. Since the freshmen had regulated matters, however, Miss Kingston had been quite affable to her when they had chanced to meet in the gymnasium.

In the growing dusk of the hall, for the maid had not yet turned on the lights, she ran plump into another girl who had just come from upstairs. "I beg your pardon," she apologized.

"Ex-cuse me!" exclaimed a familiar voice. Blame the maid for no light, but never yours truly. And where may you be hurrying to, Miss Marjorie of the Deans?"

"Oh, is that you, Leila? I didn't know you in the dark until you spoke."

"Nor I you," returned Leila. "I have been to your room twice looking for you. I was just going back to see if Miss Remson knew where you were. Ronny is in my room. I am needing you there, too. Will you come up with me now?" Leila turned toward the stairs.

"Certainly, I will. What has happened, Leila?"

"Nothing, dear heart. Only Vera and I have something to talk over with you and Ronny." Leila spoke in the friendliest kind of tones. Marjorie followed her up the stairs to the third floor where Leila and Nella Sherman roomed. Nella was absent, but Vera and Ronny greeted their entrance with expressions of satisfaction.

"I had the good fortune to bump into Marjorie in the hall," Leila said, as she ranged herself beside Marjorie, who had taken a seat on Leila's couch bed. "Now for the talk I must give you. Some of it will make you laugh and some of it will not. May I ask you, Ronny, do you spell your name L-y-n-n or L-i-n-d?"

"Neither way. It is spelled L-y-n-n-e," responded Ronny. It is an old English name."

Leila and Vera both broke into laughter. Marjorie and Ronny regarded them with mild wonderment.

"Oh, my gracious! Did you know, Ronny, that the thick-headed Sans call you Lind? They are walking about on the campus proclaiming that you are a poor Swedish servant girl who lived with the principal, Miss Someone, I have not the name, of Sanford High School. She pays your expenses here. You are not much, Ronny, so never think you are." Again Leila broke into laughter. Do poor Swedish servant girls have imported gowns of gray chiffon? I am remembering one of yours."

"They do not, as a rule." Ronny's whole face was alive with mirth. "Now who could have started that absurd tale?" She turned to Marjorie.

"I don't know." Marjorie looked troubled. Incidental with Leila's recital, Jerry's remarks concerning being "looked up" by the Sans had returned to her. "Part of that amazing information must have come from some one in Sanford who wanted to be malicious. Not the Lind part. That *is* funny." Her sober features relaxed into an amused smile. "You had better explain to the girls about the servant girl part, Ronny."

"O-h-h!" sighed Ronny. "You tell them, please, Marjorie."

"All right; glad to." Marjorie's revelation of the part Ronny had played during the previous year at high school was received with absorbed attention. When she went on to say that Ronny's father was Alfred Lynne, the noted western philanthropist, Leila gave a sharp little whistle of surprise.

"Oh, the poor Sans!" she chuckled. "Might not your father be able to buy out all their fathers and still have a dollar left?"

"He might," emphasized Ronny, with a companion chuckle. "I haven't made a secret of my identity this year. Oh, those simpletons! Well, I shall not disabuse them of their beliefs concerning me. Let them hug them to their hearts if they choose."

"That is not all, girls." Leila's features grew suddenly grave. "The rest has to do with you, Marjorie. We can't get at it. A sophomore friend of ours told Vera and me this. She asked us to pass it on to you. The Sans are talking you over among the upper class girls. Those who will listen, I mean. Our friend heard it from a soph who is about half snob, half democrat. One of the Sans received a letter from someone who seems to know all about your town and you, Marjorie. The letter is making mischief. There is something against your high school record in it. We have found out that much. We believe in you. We would like to know what you wish done concerning it."

As Leila continued speaking, Marjorie had turned very white. It was the white of righteous wrath. "There is only one person I know in Sanford who would write such a letter," she said, her voice thick with anger. "I mean Rowena Farnham, Ronny. How she happens to be in touch with the Sans I do not know. It isn't surprising. She is ill-bred, unfair and untruthful; a girl, who, without knowing me, tried to make trouble for me on her very first day at high school. I will find out who has that letter and make the person read it to me. Then I shall post a notice on the bulletin board saying that an untruthful, injurious letter is being circulated at Hamilton about me. I will not allow such a letter to gain headway!" Her tones rose in passionate protest.

"Easy, now. Don't worry." Leila's hand, warm and re-assuring, closed over Marjorie's clenched fingers. "You can't make the Sans give up the letter, Marjorie. The ring king of 'em has it. Leslie Cairns is carrying this outrage on. I believe you are right about this Farnham person. Where is she now?"

"At boarding school, I suppose. She went away to school last year. The Farnhams have a cottage at the sea shore. It is about ten miles from Severn Beach. That's where the Macys always go. Maybe Miss Cairns met Rowena there," Marjorie speculated. "I am going to tell you the whole story of my trouble with Rowena Farnham. Then you will see for yourselves the sort of a person she is."

It was a long story Marjorie had to tell. It was listened to with deep interest. Ronny had already heard the details of it from her God-mother.

"Whatever she has said against me she has made up. That doesn't remedy things; just to know yourself that it is all untrue," she concluded almost piteously. "I didn't wish such troubles to creep into my college life like hideous snakes."

"It remedies matters when you have some one to fight for you," asserted Ronny, her gray eyes steely with purpose. "I am going to make an ally of Miss Remson. Now this is my plan. I shall ask her to notify all the students that she wishes them to come to the living room at a certain time, on a certain evening. They will all respond for they will think it is something concerning their own welfare. Then I shall rise and lay down the law. You won't need to resort to the bulletin board, Marjorie. We will quash the whole thing right in the living room of Wayland Hall."

"That will be best," nodded Vera. "Miss Remson will be there and she won't stand any nonsense from the Sans. She doesn't need to accept their applications for rooms at the Hall next year."

"Well they know it," put in Leila. "Remember we shall all be there to support you, Ronny. We will rage like lions at your command."

"I shall not need it. I mean I can forge through alone. I shall love your support." Ronny's face had taken on the old mysterious expression. Too much engrossed in her own sense of injury, Marjorie did not notice this.

"My advice to you, Marjorie, is—act as though you had never seen any of the Sans when you meet them, counseled Vera. "The sooner we can call the house together the better. It is easier to spread scandal than to crush it. We must lose no time."

"This is Monday," mused Ronny. "Friday night will be best, I think."

"That is late, Ronny," objected Leila. Marjorie also regarded her chum with somber anxiety.

"It must be then," Ronny made firm reply. "Trust me in this. I have my own reasons for setting the date for Friday. There is one little item in my plan that I am not going to speak of just yet. All I can say is that it will be of great help when the time comes."

CHAPTER XXVII.

THE SECOND VICTORY.

THAT particular week seemed the longest to Marjorie she had ever spent. While she could only guess that the damaging letter held by Leslie Cairns was from Rowena Farnham, she was quite positive that there was no one else who would be mean-spirited enough to write it. Her high school record entirely clear, still it would have to be proven. She had been villified by Rowena, and lies about her published among the students of Hamilton. Unchecked, there was no telling how wide a circulation it might gain.

Jerry, who had been told of the trouble, was ready to descend upon the entire college and vanquish it single-handed. Muriel and Lucy were no less incensed. As for Miss Remson, she was for vindication on Friday night. Being as shrewd as she was good, she merely posted a notice on the house board requesting every student at the Hall to meet her in the living room at eight o'clock on Friday evening. All attempts to find out from her the nature of the meeting were fruitless. She kept her own counsel. The Sans, not wishing to curtail their chances for next year's accommodations, prudently decided to attend in a body.

"It is better to meet her, girls," Natalie Weyman urged. "She won't keep us long. She has some idiotic bee in her bonnet that is aching to buzz. We had best humor her."

"It isn't my policy to humor anyone," objected Leslie Cairns.

"Except Lola Elster," cut in Natalie with jealous sarcasm.

"That will be about all from you," retorted Leslie, insolence animating her heavy features.

"Oh, really!" flashed back Natalie, ready for battle. "How long since you acquired any authority over me?"

"Forget it," advised Joan Myers wearily. "All you two have done this evening is quarrel. I thought we were to meet in Nat's room for a good time, not a general row."

"Nat is to blame," muttered Leslie. "Let her be a little less waspish and I will try to get along with her. This is no time for us to fuss. I have been a good friend to Nat. She forgets that."

"I don't," icily contradicted Natalie. "Only I

won't take dictation from my father and mother, let alone my friends."

"Drop it, then, and listen to me." Leslie still continued to dictate, but in a modified tone. This was not lost on Natalie. She bore it, however, in discreet silence. "It is time to start on that Dean girl. I mean, to do some talking. We must catch her out on the campus and rag her a little. Leave it to me. I know how to begin on her. The rest of you, who happen to be along, can join in. Notice what I say and how I say it."

By the merest chance, Marjorie's path did not cross that of the Sans during the early part of the week. On Wednesday, after classes, she saw a number of them far down the drive, hurrying toward the Hall. Within a few yards of the steps, she entered the house and was opening the door of her room when she heard their voices in the lower hall. She tried not to think of the blight which hung over her, but she could not throw off a sense of heavy-heartedness such as she had not experienced since the time when Lucy Warner had chosen to disbelieve her word. Of all her chums, Lucy longed most to help her. She was understanding now how much her disbelief had made Marjorie suffer. Nothing could be done until Friday night, and the work of clearance lay in Veronica's capable hands.

Friday dawned, clear and sunshiny. Marjorie hailed the day with relief. That evening would end her suspense. It was time it ended, she thought. She had received signs of what might lead to partial coventry on the part of a number of upper class students. She mentally set them down as girls whom she would take a just pleasure in avoiding, later on, when the smudge had been erased from her escutcheon.

From Ronny she had learned that Miss Remson expected a full attendance in the living room that evening. The brisk little manager was up in arms at the affair and declared that she would lend every effort to stamp out the rumor. "These young women are becoming insufferable," she confided to Ronny. "Between you and me, they are not going to room at Wayland Hall next year unless the management should change hands."

On Friday afternoon Marjorie hurried from the laboratory, where she had been at work during the last recitation period of the afternoon, and set off at a rapid walk across the campus. Her hands were stained from experimentations, and she was anxious to bathe and dress for the evening before dinner. She had thought of wearing a dark green cloth gown, fur-trimmed, as the most inconspicuous dress she owned. She was greatly depressed at the idea of being dragged again into prominence. Never-

theless, no one could have persuaded her not to go
on and thresh the matter out with those who had
sought to injure her.

Influenced by her thoughts, her face showed a
sternness which seldom visited it. A fairly strong
east wind which had risen and blew against her
caused her to bow her head to it a trifle. En-
wrapped in her somber reflections, she was over
half way to the Hall when the sound of voices
smote her ears. Looking up quickly, she saw a
bevy of girls coming toward her. She recognized
them as Sans. More, that she was their objective.
She could not avoid them, nor did she wish to do
so. She simply kept on walking until within a few
feet of them.

"Steady there, Joan!" suddenly drawled a voice
Marjorie knew and disliked. "Be careful. Don't
walk over the college beauty. Why, *good afternoon,* Miss Bean! Oh, I beg your pardon; Dean, I
believe is correct. A fine day, isn't it? I imagine
it is much colder in Sanford. A fine little town, I
hear. It has such a splendid high school. One has
to have a high standard of honor to be admitted to
it. If one cheats in examinations or does anything
dishonest one is expelled from school. Just like
that!" Leslie struck her hands smartly together.
"One really should be very careful. Even if one
has been expelled and then happened to get back

into this wonderful high school, through influence, the story of one's dishonesty is likely to travel into college."

"Yes, I have heard that, too," chimed in Natalie Weyman. "We should be delighted to hear your opinion, Miss Dean. Don't be in a hurry. We have been told that you can make the prettiest little speeches. Make a speech now."

"Speech! Speech!" chorused the others, simulating avid enthusiasm. Very innocently they drew nearer, as though partially to hem her in.

"Oh, she *doesn't care* to make a speech now, girls," sneered Dulcie Vale. "Too bad! We really ought to take her down to the Colonial and blow her off to one of our real dinners. I doubt if you could get one like these specials to the San Soucians in Sanford. We haven't yet had the honor of escorting the college beauty about the campus."

"She has *so* many studies," sighed Leslie Cairns, "and with committee meetings and team work, too, her valuable time is *just simply all taken up!* What I would advise, Miss Bean; no, Dean, is a little less interest in——"

Up to this point Marjorie had listened with calm serenity to the Sans' attempts to follow out an old English school custom of "ragging." The instant she noted the change from sarcasm to belligerence in Leslie Cairns' tones, she became ready to speak and act.

"How utterly silly you all are," she said with the utmost composure. "You have no wish to know me. I have no wish to know you. As for the things you are attempting to insinuate against me, what possible harm in the end can such untruths do? Good afternoon."

Her steady brown eyes turned searchingly on her tormentors for an instant, Marjorie made a detour, passed the momentarily speechless group and continued steadily across the campus.

"What?" Leslie Cairns uttered her usual expression blankly. "What?" she said again. This time with growing displeasure.

"Well, I never!" exclaimed Natalie Weyman's high cold voice. "Of all the insolence! One might think we were peasants and she a princess!"

"Why didn't somebody say something before she got away?" demanded Joan Myers wrathfully. "I was speechless when she said that about our being silly. She might as well have called us all liars."

"Are you sure your friend Rowena is right about that high school trouble, Les?" Natalie anxiously inquired.

"Yes, she is," Leslie snapped, irritated out of her customary drawl. "She saw the whole thing. Then this Dean girl tried to lay it to her. Her father was so enraged over it that he took Rowena out of high school and sent her to Miss Alpine's School for Girls. That is an expensive school, too. The Farnhams have millions. You ought to see their place at Tanglewood! An English duke built the house and then went broke. It's a humming little palace, I will say. Cost a millon at least."

"Is that so?" returned several impressed sattelites, who, while eligible to the Sans, could not boast of million dollar summer homes, built by English dukes.

"Why don't you invite your friend Rowena down here for a day or so, Les?" asked Dulcie Vale. "It would be good sport to see her and that little Dean prig meet. I am so furious to think we let her stand there and have her say without simply extinguishing her before she had said three words."

"Oh, yes; this is a nice time to tell it," grumbled Leslie. "Why didn't you do it while you had the opportuinty?"

"Why didn't you?" pertly queried Lita Stone. "You had the same opportunity."

"What?" Leslie cast a withering look at Lita, then deliberately turned her back on the questioner and began talking to Natalie in an undertone. She had not given up her intention to continue to rag Marjorie. Next time, she planned, she would dispense with the company of all but Natalie and

Dulcie. The three of them would not bungle matters.

As for Marjorie, the reaction had set in. Divided between anger and the nervous shock attending the sudden attack, she trembled a little as she continued her way to the Hall. She was glad that she was to be cleared of the shadow that night. If Ronny had not insisted on taking up the cudgels for her, she would have braved Leslie Cairns in the latter's room and fought her own fight for honor.

Not knowing that Natalie Weyman was jealous of her, Marjorie resolved to look her prettiest, with a view toward exasperating the vain sophomore. In her wardrobe hung a frock she had not yet worn at Hamilton. It was a one-piece frock of fine wisteria-colored broadcloth which her captain had designed and made. It had a wide bertha, cuffs and over panels of wisteria panne velvet. The velvet was further beautified by a two inch appliće of silk violets on an old gold background. It was the most becoming of her afternoon gowns, and stunning enough to make the Sans wonder if it were imported.

She reached her room to find Jerry out. She sat down limply in one of the easy chairs. After ten minutes of absolute quiet, she felt better and rose to prepare for the evening in her usual methodical manner. An hour later Jerry entered to find Marjorie, looking exceptionally charming, seated at the table, deep in her trigonometry therems for next day's class.

"You look *perfectly* sweet, Marjorie," was Jerry's honest praise. "I'm glad you chose that dress. I was afraid you wouldn't dress up much. I am going to wear that dark blue velvet gown you like so well. It's my best outside my evening dresses. Ronny is going to wear her black taffeta. You know how stunning she is in black. I haven't seen Muriel today, and I don't know what Lucy will wear. I know that frozen expression of hers will be there. If it doesn't scare the Sans it ought to. I must hustle along to get togged out before dinner."

It took Jerry until the last minute before the bell rang to dress for the momentous evening. She and Marjorie went down to dinner without the latter having told her of the afternoon's disagreable occurrence. When the Five Travelers sat down at their table there was a peculiar gleam of satisfaction in Ronny's eyes. She had the air of one who had accomplished something which greatly pleased her.

"I had a little trouble with the Sans this afternoon," Marjorie quietly informed her chums as they began their dessert. She had waited until this moment rather than distract their attention from the substantial part of the dinner. "I wish you would come to Jerry's and my room after we leave the dining room. You ought to know of it before we meet the rest of the students in the living room. I hope those Sans will all be there." Into her eyes leaped stern resentment of the afternoon's insults.

"Miss Remson thinks they will all be on hand," Muriel replied. "Oh, won't I enjoy watching their faces when they hear why she called them together!"

"They may turn on you Ronny, and me, too," warned Marjorie. "If they do, don't give way a particle to them."

Ronny smiled on Marjorie in the rare wonderful fashion she so loved. "You don't know what a good fighter I am," she returned. "Wait until you see my defenses."

There was no sign of a smile on Ronny's face when she listened with the others to Marjorie's recital of the Sans ill-bred act of the afternoon. Her face registered an austerity which gave her the expression of an offended deity. Jerry and Muriel sputtered angrily over it and Lucy's green eyes gleamed threateningly enough to promise any of the offenders, who chanced to meet their concentrated stare, an uncomfortable moment.

"It is five minutes to eight." Jerry pointed to the clock. "Let's go down. On where victory points the way!" she declaimed humorously.

"And it will be victory," said Veronica, with a

sureness of tone that was vastly comforting to Marjorie.

She walked down the stairs and into the living room with Veronica. Lucy, Muriel, Katherine Langly and Jerry were directly in their wake. Chairs from the dining room had been brought into the living room and placed in regular rows facing the west wall. These chairs were already occupied by the house students. Of the thirty-six girls who lived at Wayland Hall, the Lookouts and Katherine were the last to enter. At the west end of the room were three chairs. Miss Remson occupied one. She was talking busily to a dark-haired, fine-featured woman who sat in the chair next to her own. The third chair was still vacant. Five of the six girls seated themselves on a large oak bench at the back of the room, which was still vacant on their arrival. Ronny walked serenely up the improvised side aisle to where Miss Remson and her guest were seated. Very demurely she slipped into the vacant chair.

A united gasp arose from four of the occupants of the oak bench as their eyes lighted upon Miss Remson's guest. A great wave of unexpected joy swept over Marjorie. She realized how much the presence of that beloved guest meant to her. She felt Lucy's hand slip into hers. The two girls clasped hands in an expression of silent thankfulness and rejoicing.

Conversation died out as Miss Remson rose to address the assemblage. Aside from Vera, Leila, Katherine and the Lookouts, no one present had an inkling of Miss Remson's purpose in calling them together.

"I wish to introduce to you Miss Archer, principal of the Sanford High School for Girls, of Sanford, New York. She has come to Hamilton College to right a wrong that has been done a student here, a most estimable young woman who lives among you at Wayland Hall. Had Miss Archer been unable to leave her work to come here, I should have seen justice done. However, as the case in hand comes so entirely under her jurisdiction, I am very glad of her presence tonight in that respect as well as the pleasure to be derived from her society."

Miss Remson resumed her chair and Miss Archer rose, a gracious, dignified figure in a dark brown broadcloth traveling gown. Speech for the time being was impossible. The students in the room, with the exception of the Sans, were applauding vigorously. The nature of Miss Archer's errand alone had aroused their finer sentiments. As for the Sans, they were in a quandary. The words "Sanford High School" and "right a wrong" pointed to trouble for some of them, at least. Natalie Weyman half rose from her chair. A sharp tug at her gown from Leslie Cairns and she resumed her seat. Common sense had warned Leslie that it was too late to run. The Sans were fairly caught.

"Sit still," she whispered. "Remson won't stand for our leaving. We must brazen this out. Pass the word along."

"I am going to tell the young women of Wayland Hall a little story," Miss Archer began in her direct fashion, when quiet was once more restored. "This story is about two girls. One of these two girls was entering her junior year at Sanford High School. The other girl wished to enter the sophomore class. The time of this occurrence which I shall relate was on the first day of high school. The girl who wished to enter the sophomore class reported to my office in order to take the entrance examinations. I chanced to be without a secretary at the time and was not in my office when the prospective sophomore entered it. While she waited for me she amused herself by going over the private papers on my desk. Among them was a set of examination papers marked 'Sophomore' which she would be obliged to take. She was interested in these and did not scruple to go over them.

"While she was engaged in this dishonesty, another girl entered the office. She was the bearer

of a note to me from her mother. Seeing the
stranger at the desk she naturally surmised her to
be my new secretary, my former secretary having
left me the previous June when she was graduated
from high school. The young woman with the
note asked the other frankly if she were not the
secretary. She did not answer the question with a
direct 'yes'; she merely smiled and made it appear
that she was. She continued to stand at the desk
as though she had permission to be there.

"Presently she engaged the junior, who was waiting for me, in conversation about an algebra problem on one of the papers. She pretended that she
was interested in the problems as review work. This
was nothing strange, as my secretary always takes
charge of the special examination papers. The
junior had long since finished algebra and was not
thinking much about the other's apparent interest
in a certain problem in quadratic equations which
she pointed out on one of the papers.

"To make a long story short the one girl tricked
the junior into showing her how to solve the problem. The junior, believing the other to be simply
amusing herself by solving a few of the printed
problems during my absence, worked out the one
for her which she could not solve. During this
time several girls entered the office. In each case
they were interviewed and sent about their business

by my supposed secretary. Rather to the surprise of the junior the other girl finally picked up the papers containing the finished problem and walked out of the office with them. Still the junior did not suspect her of trickery. She continued to wait for me. I did not return to the office for some time after that and she left without seeing me."

Miss Archer went on to tell of the trouble which had ensued as a result of the junior having learned that the girl she had talked with was not the secretary. Also of her own misjudgment of the innocent junior. She told of the anonymous report of the affair sent her in a letter which had been written by one of the students who had seen the two at work over the problem and misjudged the junior as being a willing party to the other's dishonesty.

Her denunciation of Rowena Farnham, for at the last she named her and Marjorie as the principals in the affair, was sharp and merciless. Her openly expressed contempt for the malicious attempt on Rowena's part to blacken Marjorie's fair name at Hamilton cut deeply into the courage of the Sans. Under the weight of evidence presented they dared not say a word. Her final remark: "My deep regard for Miss Dean as a former pupil and personal friend has made it a pleasure for me to come to Hamilton to defend her integrity," was received with acclamation on the part of Marjorie's loyal supporters.

When Ronny could make herself heard she rose and said: "I wish it understood by all present that I am the person responsible for Miss Archer's presence here tonight. No one except Miss Remson and Miss Warner knew that I had sent for her. I would like also to say that my name is *Lynne,* not *Lind,* and that I am not Swedish, but English. Any reports concerning me I should prefer to have authentic. That's all." Ronny left her station and sought the oak bench where Marjorie sat quietly crying, her head against Jerry's plump shoulder.

Following Ronny's example more than half of the assemblage left their seats and made for Marjorie. Under their warm expressions of sympathy and loyalty, her tears soon disappeared. The lesser portion of the students made their exit the moment they conveniently could, hoping not to attract too much attention. Going directly to their rooms, they came forth again in hats and coats, leaving the Hall by twos and threes. An indignation meeting at the Colonial was their objective. For once Leslie Cairns was out of favor all around for having accepted the word of her friend, Rowena Farnham, against Marjorie, without having been sure of her ground.

While the Sans were engaged in one of their futile altercations Miss Remson, assisted by the two maids, was engaged in passing around strawberry ice cream and thick-layered chocolate cake to Marjorie and her supporters.

"We have won our second victory for democracy!" exclaimed Leila triumphantly from her place on the oak bench beside Marjorie. She had made Jerry give it to her. Miss Archer sat at her beloved pupil's other side.

"I can't be sorry it happened now," Marjorie said happily. "It brought me my Miss Archer. Besides it is a *real* victory. We have shown those trouble makers, thanks to Ronny, first of all, that we are not going to be talked about at their pleasure."

"They certainly slid out of here in a hurry," commented Jerry. "They didn't dare stay."

"They did not," agreed Leila. "They will not be bothering us for some time to come. They will have to hunt well for trouble. Now, with spring here, they will be motoring and forgetting us for awhile. Do not believe they are done forever. Leslie Cairns will try again if she sees her chance. We may not see much of them the rest of this year, but look out for them as juniors. The poor, simple earth will not hold them."

"Really, I don't know where the year has gone," sighed Muriel Harding. "We are almost into the spring term and it seems to me that I haven't been here but a few weeks. We were going to try to find out a lot about the founder of this college, Brooke Hamilton. Have any of you ever looked up his history outside of what it says of him in the college bulletin?"

"I tried to find more about him at the library, but the librarian said there wasn't a single thing about him there that was of any importance. He didn't appear in books, I suppose, because he was a private gentleman. I would love to go to Hamilton Arms some time. His private library is there, they say, just as it was in his time. If we were allowed to look through it, we might find out a little about him from his collection of books. His tastes and so on, I mean." Marjorie spoke with the eagerness she always betrayed when on the subject of Brooke Hamilton. Never in a student had the departed philanthropist possessed a more generous admirer.

"If that is your heart's desire, I will be the one to tell you it is not easily obtained. A niece of his, a very old lady, lives there. She will see no one. She is not in sympathy with the college. They say she has no liking for girls," was Leila's dampening information.

"Then there is no use in sighing for the unattainable," smiled Marjorie. "Oh, well, I can keep on admiring his traditions, anyway, and help, as much as I can, to keep them green at Hamilton."

When the little feast of rejoicing was over and the Loyalites, as Leila named the participants, had sought their rooms, Marjorie's earnest words, "and help, as much as I can, to keep them green at Hamilton," rang in their ears. Each vowed in her heart to do likewise.

How Marjorie left her freshman estate behind, and traveled on into the broader realm of the sophomore, will be narrated in "MARJORIE DEAN, COLLEGE SOPHOMORE."

THE END.

The Boy Troopers Series

BY CLAIR W. HAYES

Author of the Famous "Boy Allies" Series.

The adventures of two boys with the Pennsylvania State Police.

All Copyrighted Titles.

Cloth Bound, with Attractive Cover Designs.

PRICE, 65 CENTS EACH.

THE BOY TROOPERS ON THE TRAIL

THE BOY TROOPERS IN THE NORTHWEST

THE BOY TROOPERS ON STRIKE DUTY

THE BOY TROOPERS AMONG THE WILD MOUNTAINEERS

For sale by all booksellers, or sent postpaid on receipt of price by the Publishers.

A. L. BURT COMPANY

114-120 East 23rd Street,　　　　　New York